MW00979515

Lanee's PROMISE

LINDA STEWART GREEAR

BRIDGE LOGOS

Alachua, FL 32615 USA

Bridge-Logos
Alachua, Florida 32615 USA

Lanee's Promise
by Linda S. Greear

Library of Congress Catalog Card Number: 2013944601
International Standard Book Number 978-1-61036-110-1

Illustrations by Brittany Scruggs

CH 07-08-13

Rosie 18

Lanee's PROMISE

DEDICATION

To all the neighbors in Highland City, Florida, USA— my village.

And to the real Lanee, Bill, Netta, Olivia, and Lorea Hope— my grandchildren.

CONTENTS

ACKNOWLEDGMENTS

GREAT thanks to my daughter, Lee Turner, for always helping any way she can. It was her idea to send off an application for a writing test for me.

I had a lot of fun taking that writing test then signed up for the course they offered me. That's where I met my instructors, Lynda Durrant and Deborah Vetter. How I wanted to write something they would like. Thanks, Lynda and Debby for teaching me. I began *Lanee's Promise* as a short story for Lynda, and then as the book project Debby asked me to do.

In the midst of the book, I questioned what the Lord thought of my spending so much time writing. My husband Michael prayed and heard the Lord say, "Encourage her!" He has ever since. Thank you, Michael. And thank you, Lord.

As I worked on *Lanee's Promise,* I read it to the women inmates of the Polk County Jail and the residents of Hawthorne Inn. Their positive comments fueled my writer's fire. Thanks, ladies and gentlemen.

Just in time, God sent me a new friend, Brittany Scruggs. She has drawn pictures to illustrate *Lanee's Promise.* Thank you, Brittany, for using your talent to add to Lanee's story.

I would also like to thank my son-in-law, Don Turner, for helping me with the writing equipment and so much more.

FOREWORD

*L*ANEE'S PROMISE is a story about someone who is like a gentle dove in this world, whom the Bible tells us not to grieve. He is the Holy Ghost. How can one write a fiction book about the person who is called the "Spirit of Truth?" I wrestled with it. Could I say He said something He never said? Could I write about characters being moved on by Him, which were not real people? I wanted to, for the story was in my heart, but would it be *right?*

Since you're holding it, you can see I have been allowed to write the story. And the Lord has helped me. Yet, I have been responsible for clinging to the truth as diligently as possible. From my own first-hand experience and the story told in God's Word, I've tried to let Lanee express to you what it is like to be filled with the Holy Ghost. I have quoted Scriptures from my tried and proven Holy Bible, and I've left them in their King James Version of the Bible language, so you can recognize them as such. Though I've never seen Jesus, I've sought to relate to you who He is through the lens of my own experiences with Him.

I hope *Lanee's Promise* will show you there's joy in being filled with the Holy Ghost. When you are filled, I hope Lanee's victory will help you face what the world thinks about it. If you've never been baptized with the Holy Ghost and fire, I hope my book will inspire you to be, and then help you reach *your* village for Jesus.

So I give you *Lanee's Promise.* Is it just a story? Or could it also be a new door swinging open for you?

Sister Linda Greear
Highland City, Florida

PROLOGUE

A TINY ant wrestled a stiff Goliath of a wasp through the blades of grass. *How?* I bent over for a closer look.

That's when I heard His voice grow louder. Worn leather sandals stepped down right beside the ant, and the voice stopped. My heart went to drumming in my ears—*He must be standing right next to me.*

I tipped my head up and froze. Steady brown eyes were waiting for mine. *Oh, my!* I was only one of the multitudes sitting in the grass, yet He was staring down at me.

I began trembling; still my mind was curious. *Could you be … are you our Messiah?*

His intense brown eyes really gripped mine then and I saw a warm feeling like pure honey pour into them—*why … He loves me!*

Me? I felt less frightened. I smiled.

I expected Him just to look away then. Instead, He gave me something—a gift only I knew how much I wanted. His beating heart reached down and touched mine, and in that thrilling moment, Heaven opened! All I could do was squeeze my eyes shut and worship. *My God! Oh my Lord God … now, I know you are real!*

Then I heard Jesus tell the people, "I and my Father are one."

I came up on my knees feeling awestruck and happy. Bowing over His dusty toes, I whispered, "My Messiah."

CHAPTER ONE

THE MESSIAH COMES

"LANEE! Lanee! Wake up!" It was Abba calling up the stone stairs from our front room. He'd lit the lamp and the golden light splashed over my walls and ceiling. "I'm awake, Abba. What is it?"

"I'm going with you and Eema out to the field today, and I need to tell Yosef. Come with me, Yonina."

He called me his dove, and he's going with us! That woke me up. I threw off the covers.

"Wait, I'm coming!" I called, reaching for my tunic. Our old rooster crowed as I slipped into the dusty sandals I'd kicked off last night. Quickly running my fingers through the tangles, I tied a scarf around my hair and hurried down the six steps to my father.

Abba was wearing his everyday robe and a quiet smile. He handed me a fold-over of Eema's bread and soft goat cheese, then blew out the lamp and opened the front door.

In the morning twilight, we walked the dirt road toward the lakeside inn where he worked. When the road turned downhill, fog colored a soft pink by the morning light rolled in toward us from the Sea of Galilee. I savored the last bite of bread and cheese as the red tiles of the inn's roof appeared. Soon we could see the whitewashed buildings perched on the lakeshore.

I breathed in the water and earth smells and gave out a loud sigh. *How happy can a fourteen-year-old girl be?*

7

Yesterday I was blessed to meet Jesus, and today my abba will get to meet Him, too!

Abba smiled down at me. "It *is* one pleasant morning, Lanee. I'm glad we're sharing it."

Our chuffing steps approached the stable yard. I got a whiff of the hay and livestock as we hurried on to the arched doorway that led to the flowered courtyard. Rounding the corner, we stopped in front of Yosef's door.

Abba kissed the top of my head and said, "Wait here, my yonina, while I talk to Yosef."

He knocked, and I heard Yosef's raspy answer, "Come in."

Too early for the guests to be up, I could choose any of the stone benches. It was one of the few times I had the *Yafe Perach* all to myself. Yosef gave his flowered courtyard that pretty name which meant Beautiful Flower. The lovely rose garden was framed in red pavement stones that made up the walkway for the whitewashed rooms of the inn.

This morning the red, pink, and yellow roses were all glorious dripping with dew. The best one, the giant bush covered in butter-colored blossoms, was showing off over there by the door to the Window Room. I imagined it a queen's fine billowing skirt embroidered with lush yellow roses.

A cool lakeside breeze sprang up. I traced its path as it stirred the fronds of the date palms that guarded the corners of the broad courtyard. Next, it nudged the lazy-looking willow switches, and hurried over to ruffle the leaves of the mulberry tree in the middle of the court. The tree's thousands of hairy green berries bounced up and down. The bench underneath its branches is my favorite spot when those berries get ripe.

8

I glanced back at Yosef's door. Abba wasn't coming yet. I was curious what Yosef thought about Abba going to see Jesus. Not that it would matter, for I knew he'd give him the day off if he could spare him. Yosef wasn't just Abba's employer; he was his friend. Abba had helped Yosef build the inn before I was born.

I imagined them sitting at Yosef's desk. Faintly I detected the smell of Yosef's room even out here. It was the odor of fried fish, of the spice mixture Yosef used in his cooking, and of the hundreds of old scrolls he owned. I remember the first time Savta borrowed one of his ancient scrolls to teach us girls the Scriptures. She removed its brocade cover, and I felt a chill run down the back of my neck—it felt like we were opening a door to the past.

Kindly Yosef was not quite as old as his scrolls, but was just as mysterious. He was the only *sabba* I ever had; though he wasn't really by birth. I wondered if Yosef wanted to meet Jesus too.

Getting impatient, I paced across the courtyard toward the dining room. The enticing fragrance of fresh bread met me. *Any minute now, they will need Yosef in the kitchen. Surely, his door will open soon.*

I peeked into the Window Room. Across the broad room furnished with oaken tables and chairs, the sunlight sparkled at me. I saw it through the glass window on that side of the room. No one else had such a thing. The expensive glass had to be brought all the way from Caesarea! Abba told me customers from everywhere came to enjoy Yosef's fried fish and the view from that wall-sized window that opened out on the lake.

I paced back toward the closed door. Falling down on a bench, I worried whether Yosef could spare Abba today. I didn't want to wait another day for him to meet Jesus.

How glad I was that Eema had ventured out just two days ago to hear Him. It was the first day He had come to the grassy hills behind our house. But we'd been hearing wonderful stories about Jesus for months—how He'd healed lepers, even caused blind people to see!

What really astounded us was what we heard about Jesus and the new prophet John the Baptist. John is a powerful preacher who gathers large crowds. One day John pointed to Jesus and said, "Behold, the Lamb of God." But, oh, my! Listen to this! When Jesus came to be baptized by him, John took Him under the water and brought Him up, and immediately a dove flew down and lit on His head. At the same moment a voice spoke out of Heaven saying, "This is my beloved Son in whom I am well pleased." Witnesses said they *actually* heard God speak from the sky. How we wanted to meet Jesus after hearing that!

That day Eema met Him, I ran home from Savta's with my mouth watering. Mmm, fresh bread, warm and delicious, and dripping with butter and fig jam. It was Eema's baking day. I barreled on through the house, but suddenly slowed when I heard Eema out by the oven doing something I'd never known her to do—she was sobbing.

"Eema, what's wrong?" I asked, afraid something had happened to Abba.

"Lanee, no, don't be afraid—I am crying for joy, not sadness. I've found Jesus. I went out on the hillside this morning where He's come to preach. I feel so happy,

Lanee, I can't keep from crying. Oh! Oh!"

Found Jesus? Crying for happiness? Oh, my! I stood there watching Eema, maybe really seeing her as a person for the first time. Sometimes I noticed how rough her hands were, for she worked all the time. Her long brown hair, usually so neatly done up, had some flyaway strands falling over her bowed face now. Tears rolled down her soft tanned cheeks and wet her tunic. How sweet she was crying over Jesus.

She soon dried her face on her apron and walked over to me. "You must come with me tomorrow, Lanee."

"Oh, yes, Eema!" I said as I hugged her, "I'd really like to."

Abba worked late that night at the inn, and somehow I don't think Eema told him about Jesus, for only the two of us went the next day. I dashed over to my grandmother's house before we went. Savta was bedfast and needed my help every morning. Finally, the bed was remade and her noon meal was ready and waiting and I ran home. Then Eema and I hurried over the wild field grass to see Jesus.

Now everything is different. Gazing at the sun topping the Window Room, waiting for Abba to reappear, I remembered the look in Jesus' eyes and the sensation of God's presence. *Oh, how different I feel!*

Last night Eema told Abba where we'd been. She told him how Jesus had preached and then said, "I believe Jesus is our Messiah, Jonathan."

Abba's eyebrows shot up! To us Jews the *Messiah* is everything. We have been looking for Him always. It is He that will deliver us from our oppressors; then we will crown Him our king.

But I knew Eema wasn't even thinking of a *conquering*

king. She said, "Jesus invited me to come to Him and find rest yesterday, Jonathan." She looked at Abba with eyes filling up with tears. "I wasn't sure what that meant, but I got up and walked toward Him. Others did the same thing, until we were thickly crowded around Him. He seemed surprised at first, then He said, 'Go in peace; your faith hath saved you.' I can't explain it," she said, "but ever since that moment I've felt happiness like I've never known." Then Eema wept again as hard as she had out by the oven.

Abba reached up and pulled her down on his knees. He knew Eema. Something rare had touched her.

I didn't say anything about Jesus right then. I just couldn't share my secret. Even though Eema was sitting right beside me when it happened, I don't think she saw how wonderfully He'd touched me.

And we'll all see Him today, if only Abba can come!

It was almost as if my yearning drew Abba out of Yosef's room. I turned at the sound of his sandals. "Yosef's fine without me today, Lanee, let's go!" he said.

I followed him, getting more excited with every step. He didn't say anything until we were outside of the courtyard and on the dirt road home.

"Yosef wants me to find out if Jesus is the Messiah. His cousin Theo witnessed God speaking from Heaven at the Jordan and told Yosef He'd never heard anything like it."

Silently I wondered what God's voice sounded like. Then I asked, "Does Yosef think Jesus is the Messiah, Abba?"

He slowed down and turned to look at me. "Maybe he does. He reminded me that the second Psalm says, 'Thou art my Son; this day have I begotten thee.' Yosef said that is much like what God said about Jesus at the River Jordan."

Abba bent down and picked up a stick. He flipped it over in his hand and flung it down the dusty road. Watching where it dropped, he said, "Later in the Psalms, the Scripture says, 'Kiss the Son, lest he be angry, and ye perish from the way when his wrath is kindled but a little.'"

"I read that once when Savta assigned us the Psalms to read. But what does it mean, Abba?"

Abba thought a minute before he said, "David seems to be telling us to love God's Son because our future happiness depends on it."

I instantly knew that was right. But Abba hadn't met Jesus yet, so he pondered it as we walked on.

When we came to the stick, he picked it up and sent it flying again. Then he said, "We've been hearing that Jesus claims to be the Son of God. Yosef is quite anxious to know if He really is."

"Abba, Jesus would make God a wonderful Son."

I felt his hand on my shoulder and stopped. I turned to look at Abba's face handsomely framed in his curly beard and brown hair. The morning sunlight revealed some gray beginning to show above his ears. He studied my eyes then started back down the road. For a few steps, it was quiet except for the sound of our feet scrunching over the sand.

"My daughter," he said tenderly, "the second Psalm ends by saying, 'Blessed are all they that put their trust in him.'" Then almost to himself, he said, "Perhaps today I am seeing what that means."

I felt a little shy when I said, "Eema has put her trust in Him, Abba, and yesterday I couldn't help believing in Him, too."

His hazel eyes found mine. "Today, *I* will know, Lanee."

Then he seemed lost in thought, and I began thinking too—*God has given us this beautiful morning; is He is also blessing us actually to meet our Messiah? All our ancestors have waited and been disappointed. But, oh my, I remember the touch of His heart and how He showed me His power with God. And if my Eema believes He is our Messiah, too, surely it must be true!*

I started running at the first glimpse of our fieldstone house.

"Eema, we're home!" I called as I ran through the cool of our front room. "Abba's going with us to see Jesus!"

She answered, "I'm out here, Lanee," and I ran to the courtyard. She looked up at me from the hot oven. Her face was all flushed. I helped her carry in the fresh barley cakes and fried eggs. As I poured the warm goat's milk into our cups, Abba came through the door.

I glanced up then looked again. An excited light danced in my abba's eyes like I'd never seen before. When I turned toward Eema, she was smiling at him and I knew what she was thinking. *Today, you, my dear Jonathan, will meet my Jesus, too!*

CHAPTER TWO

ABBA MEETS HIS MESSIAH

FTER breakfast, I left for Savta's, hoping she was in a good mood.

"It's me, Savta," I called as I walked through her front room into her bedroom. "How did your night go?"

"I hurt terribly all night, Lanee. Come and rub between my shoulders before this pain drives me out of my mind."

When I finished her back rub, I hurried through my other chores. My mind wasn't on the floor I swept, or the food I prepared. I was out in the grass, listening to Jesus, with Abba beside me.

"Savta, may I go now? I've laid out your lunch and made sure everything is clean." She was resting on fresh linens and her hair was combed nicely.

"Why are you in such a rush again today, Lanee?" She frowned up at me from her cushions. "You know I like you to keep me company." I noticed how much her face was like Abba's, only with more wrinkles, and less cheer.

"Well ... uh ... Abba is not working today, and we're ... uh ... going out in the fields in a little while." I didn't want to tell Savta we were going to see Jesus. Somehow, I knew she wouldn't like it. Since she'd been sick, the slightest thing made her angry.

"Your abba not working?" She picked up her linen sheet

and shook it. "Jonathan always works every day but the Sabbath! What's going on?"

Meekly, I answered, "We are going out where ... where Jesus will be."

"What?" Savta's face turned deep red and her eyes flashed. "Did you say Jesus? The carpenter's son from Nazareth?" I'd heard her speak of rats in a sweeter tone. She frowned at me for a very long minute and then mumbled something I couldn't hear. "Well ... tell your abba I need to talk to him just as soon as you get back!"

"Yes, Savta." I gave her a parting kiss on one hard cheek and scrambled out the door. I felt her scowl follow me all the way home.

When I told Abba what she said, he didn't seem worried. In fact, I thought he was about to break out in a grin. He said, "You eat your food, Yonina, and we'll be ready to go."

At certain times, my abba is a comical person. As I said before, he has a wide face covered with a soft dark beard. He also has ears that stick out from his head. That sounds like he's not handsome, but, oh my, he is! His eyes are green and brown with gold thrown into the mix. (They say my eyes are like his.) When he is amused, excited, or even challenged, that look comes across his face. It starts in his eyes, then spreads over his face, and finally pulls his wide mouth open for a joyous grin. When I saw it happening about what Savta said, I stopped worrying about her opinion.

I don't recall *what* I ate for the noon meal for I was impatient to go. Finally, we left through the back gate of our courtyard. We waded through calf-high grass, listening only to the *swish-swish-swishing* of our clothes against a background rhythm of buzzing insects. Our feet stirred up the good smell of crushed Galilean grass and the warm earth.

I ran ahead and whirled around to walk backwards. Abba and Eema were holding hands. Abba's face was tan and shining, and Eema's lips held a compressed smile. We all had on our everyday homespun clothes, but Eema had added a soft scarf around her hair, and Abba wore his Sabbath linen cloak. I had on my best striped kerchief knotted under my long hair.

Letting them catch up to me, I took Abba's other hand. If I were ten, I'd skip and sing, *"We're bringing Abba to see Jesus!"* But I turned fourteen many months ago, so I decided not to. I remember that day. We'd wandered in this same field until we found just the right spot to spread my birthday supper. Today many others were along for our ramble, but this time we were going out to see Jesus, the Son of God. That was much better than a birthday.

We caught up to a family who were talking loudly about Him. The tall man with long legs was saying, "I tell you, Jonas, He can't be what He claims to be. He's an uneducated peasant."

"Just you wait until you hear Him, Cyrus," answered the shorter man hurrying to keep up. "You'll change your mind."

Abba greeted the men. They weren't from our village, but we saw many who were. I recognized Deborah far ahead of us. She was holding the arm of her enormous bodyguard, one of her father's slaves. Her long black hair swayed rhythmically across her back.

Soon we were just about there. "Do you remember when we ate my birthday supper out here, Abba?" I said looking up at him. "Yesterday Jesus stood on the very spot you chose for our picnic."

"Is that so?" he said as we topped the hill.

An amazing sight lay before us. Multitudes of people were gathered there—even more than yesterday. Glancing toward Abba, I saw he was impressed. Finally the moment had come. What would Abba think of Jesus?

I watched him scan the crowd. When he narrowed his eyes, I knew he'd located the disciples—Jesus' twelve chosen followers. I looked there too, catching my breath when I saw Jesus step out into the open. A linen cloth draped over His head shielded Him from the hot sun. I quickly turned back to see Abba's expression. His eyes had grown wide. What did I see stealing over my father's face? Was it *awe*? Tears sprang up in my eyes.

"Let's move up close." he said, and then pulled on our hands. Down we went into the crowd. My abba is a man who *will* provide. Soon we were sitting on his cloak under the shade of a bushy myrtle tree. About as far away as Abba could throw that stick this morning, was the one we'd come to see. We had a perfect view of Him, His disciples, and possibly a hundred sick people lying on mats all around Him.

"Yesterday there weren't any people on mats, Eema. Why are they here?"

"Earlier today, Sylvia told me that Jesus healed a blind man's eyes after we left yesterday," Sylvia is our neighbor and Eema's good friend. "I guess when others heard about it, they came to be healed, too."

Sitting up on my knees, I gazed at the sick people. They were on every kind of bed with all sorts of coverings, from clean sheets to filthy burlap bags. Most of them lay with their arms over their eyes shielding them from the bright sun. They'd probably not been outside for a long time.

Across from us, I saw Deborah. I started to wave, and then remembered yesterday. She'd acted embarrassed that I'd seen her here. Her grown up brother Joel was with her then. Today sitting beside the huge slave guardian, she looked almost like a small doll. I wondered how it felt to have servants. I would probably never know. I also wondered why she came back.

Yesterday Rabbi ben Tzadik, the ruler of our synagogue, had also come. Like Deborah, he'd acted uncomfortable, and today he was nowhere to be seen.

I scanned every group for Ben. *Not here.* I was disappointed. He'd come with his abba yesterday. How my heart had pounded when I saw his bushy black hair and dark eyes. I'd tried not to let him see me looking his way, and I guess I'd succeeded. He hadn't noticed me.

Jesus removed His head covering and began walking among the mats. The crowd quieted down. Today I noticed how young He was, younger than I expected someone so renowned to be—years younger than Abba. In fact, more *ordinary* looking than I expected, too. He was tan, with the sun-bleached hair and beard of one of Yosef's field laborers. Wearing a linen tunic and a girdle of the same fabric, His looks and speech were as common as Abba's and most of the others' in the crowd. But yesterday, I learned that He was no ordinary man. Jesus *knew* God. He was close enough to Him to help me to know Him. Not even Abba could do that. I sensed Jesus was through and through clean, and apart from us. Perhaps I mean *holy. Oh, Jesus!*

He stopped at a mat with a small boy on it. The boy was crying and holding his stomach. His thin face was rosy with fever. The boy's eema and abba, standing beside the mat, cried when Jesus walked their way. He laid His hand on the boy's stomach and spoke some quiet words. I watched the boy stop crying, then he relaxed and fell asleep right out there in the bright sunshine. His eema and abba wept more as they thanked Jesus.

Jesus approached a man whose nose had been eaten off by disease. It bothered me to look at him—what had been his nose were two open holes surrounded by gray oozing matter. Jesus touched him and spoke softly. I held my breath in anticipation.

Suddenly I saw the miracle begin. As naturally as the sky fills up with clouds, I saw his face fill up with a new nose. How could it be? Yet it seemed so simple! The grizzled old man felt it happening and reached up to touch his new nose. He even looked cross-eyed to see if his desire had really come. I looked over at Abba. I could see his grin coming on.

We watched Jesus go among the mats healing a blind eye,

a broken foot, a face full of sores, a bad knee. Many suffering old people waited to be noticed. Jesus touched them, and the women sat up, trying to fix their hair, while the men smiled and talked with their friends and family in the crowd.

Jesus moved to a mat where a woman lay. I could see her body curved awkwardly under the sheet. Her hands were claws, and her eyes looked frightened. Again, Jesus spoke quietly. Her eyes swam with tears. We heard bones popping and cracking, and all at once, she stood up! She was the skinniest person I'd ever seen. Her tunic bagged everywhere.

Eema shocked me by jumping up, "Oh, Zia! It's you! What a great thing!" she cried.

The skinny woman recognized her, "Cilla! Oh, Cilla, look! Jesus has healed me!" she rejoiced. They came together hugging and laughing.

Jesus lifted up a lame man. Suddenly the lame man took off running. Around the whole perimeter of the crowd he ran, crying, "Look at me run! Look at me run!"

That's when we started shouting! What an experience! Mix up joy, surprise, and excitement, and let it loose from a thousand throats! Jesus healed, and we shouted. Jesus healed some more, and we shouted louder.

"It is He!" declared Abba with tears in his eyes. Then he shouted, "Lord Jesus!"

CHAPTER THREE

JESUS SPEAKS TO ME

I 'VE never spent an afternoon like that. Healing flowed freely out of Jesus' hands. Those who were healed gathered up their mats and waited to see the next miracle Jesus would do. We were awed to silence by the time the last little girl got up and walked. Her eema cried, "Oh, Jesus, you have healed my crippled baby's legs!"

Appearing exhausted, Jesus motioned for His disciples to send us home. I peered back over my shoulder. Our worn-out Jesus stood alone, watching us leave. The image burned into my heart.

Voices woke me in the night. Abba and Eema must have used the outside stairs to reach the half-walled rooftop beside my bedroom. I heard them weeping out toward the grassy spot where Jesus had preached and healed.

The low rumble was Abba's voice. "We've met our Messiah—He's finally come!"

Softer was Eema's teary reply, "Oh, Jonathan, we are so blessed!"

Quiet sobbing reached my ears for a while then the muffled slapping of sandals on the steps told me I was alone again. It was no use trying to go back to sleep. Over and over I tossed, as questions ran through my mind. *How can Jesus be our Messiah? Our Messiah is supposed to be a mighty warrior, like David or Samson. He is a king—not like what Savta said—a lowly carpenter from Nazareth. He is supposed to deliver us from the oppressing Romans and all their cruelties. But that just doesn't sound like Jesus!* I tried hard to imagine Jesus fighting a Roman soldier. It was impossible.

Could the Messiah be different than we had always supposed? Could He have come not to fight, but to *love?* I thought how Jesus' eyes spoke His love, and how His heart touching mine opened up a direct connection to God. Could He have come just to bring us God's love? And the joy of feeling His touch? *Oh, Jesus.*

We were so glad He preached several more days in our fields. The next day I helped Savta early in the morning then left in a hurry for home. My savta gave me a frozen look when I went toward the door, but didn't comment. Eema and I went ahead to get a good spot; Abba would come later when he could leave the inn. We arrived in time to spread our blanket over the prickly grass not far from where Jesus usually stood. It was a while before the meeting would start.

"Eema, do you think Jesus would speak to me if I went to Him?" I asked as I waved away the gnats attacking my face.

Her eyes lit up, but replied, "You see how everyone wants His attention, Lanee." Then she turned her eyes in His direction, "Go ahead, and try it."

What will I say? Will He remember me? I trudged toward Him through the trampled grass. Up close, I heard what He was telling His disciples, "Suffer the little children to come unto me, and forbid them not, for of such is the Kingdom of God." All at once, the men standing between Jesus and me moved, and I walked right into the little flock of children and eemas that surrounded Jesus.

Jesus lifted a small girl into His lap, laid His hands on her, and said, "Father, bless her to love you." He put her down and lifted another one. I was the only one too big to sit in His lap, which made me worry a little. Finally, He looked up at me with recognition, and stood. He placed His hands on my head and said, "Go into all the world, Lanee, and preach to the little ones of my love, and I will be with you." He gazed warmly into my eyes. Again.

"Yes, Lord," I smiled and put all my heart into adding, "Thank you."

When I told Eema what He said, we both cried.

Abba managed to work early and get there in the afternoons to hear Jesus. He'd go back and work in the evenings to make up for the missed time. When we were all set, Eema and I watched for him. I loved turning around at just the right time to spy my hot-faced abba swooping in for a landing on our blanket, most of the time just before Jesus began His message.

When Jesus preached, sometimes I gazed at His hands. They were tanned by the sun, and He moved them as my father moves his hands. Practiced by work, Abba would say. Jesus spoke in a strong voice that carried to the men far back in the crowd, but never seemed too loud to me up front. One day He said, "Verily, verily I say unto you, I am the door of the sheep. All that ever came before me are thieves and robbers: but the sheep did not hear them. I am the door: by me if any man enter in, he shall be saved, and shall go in and out, and find pasture."

I glanced at Eema and saw by her gentle smile that she was enjoying the picture He painted of her being a trusting sheep in His care. Abba chewed on a grass stem, as he listened on the other side of me. I looked back at Jesus' expressive hands.

"I am the good shepherd," Jesus said. "The good shepherd will give His life for the sheep."

What? Did He say He would give His life? My eyes flew up to His.

His eyes traveled over the crowd as He continued His message, "I lay down my life for the sheep."

Oh, what did you say, Lord? Will you lay down your life? I stared at Him, wondering why He said such things.

As we made our way home that afternoon, I asked Abba, "What did Jesus mean when He said He will give His life for the sheep?

He shook his head, "I don't know, Lanee. I guess we'll just have to wait and see."

All that week we tried to get Savta to go with us and be healed, but she called it foolishness and wouldn't go. She didn't think the Messiah would be a "country preacher."

The day before the Sabbath, we heard that overnight Jesus had moved across the lake. Suddenly a hollow place opened inside of me—how I was going to miss Him! To encourage myself, I thought, *Maybe He'll come back this way.*

After He was gone, I found believing in Him was still a cause for excitement. At supper, we would remember the miracles and try to recall all He'd taught us. Once Abba spoke up, "Remember Him saying, 'He that believeth on me hath *everlasting* life?'" The three of us were feeling it!

In our village of Arbela, Jesus' name was on everyone's lips, though not because everyone loved Him. I saw that clearly the afternoon Elisabeth, Misha, and I were at the well filling our water jugs. As we worked, we chattered excitedly about the latest news we'd heard about Jesus. He'd brought a twelve-year-old girl back to life!

That's when Sarah and Deborah arrived.

Elisabeth's long braids fell over her shoulders as she called out from her seat on the well, "Just *guess* what Jesus has done now, Sarah." She flipped her braids back and jumped down to help me raise the full bucket of water.

"No, I don't want to!" Sarah fussed, setting her water pot down on the ground. "I'm tired of hearing about Jesus!" she said and gave me one of her meanest looks.

Like father, like daughter. Our rabbi didn't allow my abba to speak in the synagogue anymore since Abba stood up and said he believed that Jesus is the Messiah. Now Sarah preached directly at me, "My abba says that man gets His power from the devil. And He's trying to fool everyone into following Him so He can be a king!"

I carefully emptied the bucket into my jug and said, "Sarah, Jesus is our Messiah." This seemed so easy to say when I remembered His hands reaching down to the sick and healing them. I could still hear the sound of Zia's bones cracking into place. And how could I ever forget the man growing a new nose? Besides, He'd even called me by name, and I'd never told it to Him.

Then Deborah spoke. "He is not accepted by our synagogue and the good men of our village. Why would you and your parents want to believe in Him?"

I looked up. She was staring off toward the setting sun as if she didn't care what I answered. Her raven hair framed her beautiful face in the twilight. She had no water pot to fill, for she was the only daughter of the wealthiest man in Arbela—Daniel ben Judah, owner of a fleet of fishing boats, large fig and olive groves, and herds of cattle and sheep. He was highly esteemed in the synagogue, for everyone knew he gave generously to the treasury.

I felt the familiar longing rise up in me. Oh, how I'd love to be close friends with Deborah—even *best* friends. Always she had chosen Sarah. I felt it pulling at me. Suddenly I was surprised by another feeling pulling back—the image of Jesus, all worn out from healing everyone, watching us all go home that day. It was then I realized I had a new best friend. And I would never trade Him to be friends with anyone—even Deborah.

"Didn't you see Him heal all those sick people, Deborah?" I asked, hoping she'd at least have to admit that.

"I can't explain what I saw, but I won't be taken in by Him."

With that, both Jesus and I were dismissed.

CHAPTER FOUR

THE GOOD SHEPHERD GIVES HIS LIFE

ACH DAY in Galilee was a little longer and a little hotter, as summer shouldered out spring. We hadn't seen Jesus since that precious week in our fields, yet Abba heard from a traveler at the inn that He'd healed ten lepers at once. News came that out in a field near another village He'd blessed seven small loaves of bread and a few little fishes and fed four thousand men besides women and children. Oh, what great power our Messiah had!

It was a busy time of the year for Abba. He worked long hours helping with Yosef's crops, as well as keeping things running smoothly at the inn.

Passover came, but we couldn't go to Jerusalem this time. Savta was too sick for us to be so far away. Eema and I alternated days helping her. Though she slept most of the time, when she was awake, I just couldn't please her. "Lanee, don't shake that rug inside. Can't you see all that dust you've stirred up?" or "You're pulling my hair out by the roots, girl! Just leave my hair alone!" she growled. I had to keep reminding myself how sweet she used to be, and that her grumpiness was only because she was ill. Would I ever have my pleasant savta back?

We ate supper at her house every evening. When Abba and I arrived one warm night after Passover, there stood my

29

handsome Dod Ethan, in the doorway holding out his arms to us. What a surprise! He was the one Savta always called "my beloved son-in-law."

"Ethan!" cried my abba, "You've come all the way from Jerusalem! Did Ruth come with you? And the boys?" He hugged Dod Ethan and kissed his cheek, with Eema smiling behind them. She had been there helping Savta all day, and was enjoying being in on the surprise.

As young men, Abba and my dod became friends in Jerusalem after meeting during Passover. Abba brought him to their Mount of Olives campsite to introduce him to the family. Ethan took one look at Abba's younger sister, sunny and sweet Ruth, and fell in love. That all happened years before I was born.

Now all wrapped up in Abba's hug, Dod Ethan said, "No, I … I didn't bring them. I … I left in a hurry."

He'd always loved visiting Eema and Abba, but sometimes he had come all the way from Jerusalem to Arbela just to see *me*. He and Dodah Ruth only had boys so I was his pet. When Abba let go of him, I hugged him around the middle.

Dod Ethan led us to Savta's room. As we followed, I noticed the luxurious robe he wore. My uncle was the successful businessman in our family. He was the owner of "Ethan's Sandals," sellers of the best shoes to be bought in Jerusalem. He didn't go to the workshop or sell in the stores anymore, for he had many hired helpers.

Eema had Savta propped up in her bed. Her gray curls were combed prettily over her pillow and I saw a new sparkle in my grandmother's eyes.

"Jonathan, isn't this a lovely treat?" She said, taking

Dod Ethan's hand in hers when he came near. "It was just what I needed to help me recover."

Dod Ethan smiled down at her then went back toward the front room. He returned with a linen bag that held gifts he'd brought along for us—three expensive pairs of sandals. I couldn't wait to try mine on. They were made out of soft tan calves skin. I slid my feet out of my old sandals and found that the new ones fit just right.

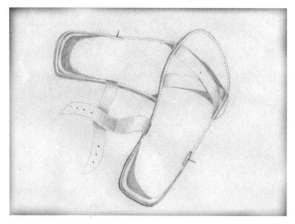

"Oh, thank you, Dod!" I got him around the neck and kissed him right in the middle of his fuzzy beard.

He hugged me back and said, "I was hoping your little feet had grown some, Lanee."

Abba smiled down at his new sandals and said, "Come Ethan, tell us the news of Jerusalem—you know we weren't there for Passover."

Abba sat on the mat and leaned back on the foot of Savta's bed and Dod Ethan sat near her pillow. I completed the circle, facing her. My grandmother was feeling happy, I could tell, from having her "boys" so close. Lying back on several comfortable pillows, her eyes were bright with anticipation of the men's talk. Eema sat near Dod Ethan and the lampstand. She seemed glad just to sit and rest after the day's work.

The room felt so cozy. We were leaning on cushions covered in shades of bright crimson and warm amber. Savta loved those colors. The woven floor mat we sat on was of split golden reeds. All of us were bathed in the soft light the oil lamp cast. I wiggled my toes in my new sandals, and smiled over at Dod Ethan who always provided them for us. It was such a golden moment of happiness. Next to me, Abba's face shone from both the lamplight and the prospect of talking with his friend again. I looked over at Eema, sitting with her eyes closed, waiting to hear the news.

"Uh … have … haven't you heard any news from Jerusalem since last week's Passover?" Dod Ethan asked with a curiously sober expression.

"No, we haven't. I've been out in the fields helping with Yosef's barley harvest, working until dark every day. What has happened?" said Abba.

"Perhaps, I should wait to tell you when we are alone, Jonathan. It is some hard news."

"Who is it about, Dod Ethan?" I couldn't help asking.

He hesitated, then turned toward me and answered, "It is concerning the one that is called Christ—Jesus of Nazareth."

Abba spoke up, "In that case, brother, you must tell us all, for He is very important to us."

I looked over at Savta. Wearing a frown, she straightened her already smooth coverlet. That was one name she never mentioned. Knowing how she felt about Jesus, I never spoke of Him to her either, though, I wanted to.

"Son, what do you mean by saying, 'He is very important

to us'?" she asked sharply.

Abba turned and spoke very firmly to his mother, "Don't you remember all I said after we met Him, Eema? I told you then, I believe in Jesus—He is our Messiah. Do you think I have changed my mind?"

Savta stared into his eyes, then closed hers and said no more.

Dod Ethan cleared his throat and looked worried.

Abba turned back to my uncle and asked, "What 'hard news' is there to tell about Jesus, Ethan?"

Dod Ethan studied the strips of the woven rug. Then he lifted his face. His lips were compressed. I noticed for the first time the dark circles under his eyes. A crease had formed between his eyebrows. I've never seen my good-humored uncle look like this.

"They ... I mean ... *we* ... uh ... *crucified* Him," he said, and stared past my shoulder.

"Crucified Him?" we cried out together. All of us but Savta, that is.

My mouth hung open in shock. Thoughts began tumbling in my head—*Jesus has been crucified? The Romans execute criminals that way. Why Jesus? He was no criminal. Why would they nail Him to a cross? Not my Messiah!*

Feeling panic, I looked at Abba, then over at Eema. Both of their mouths hung open and their eyes were wide with shock from Dod Ethan's words.

No. It can't be true. Jesus can't be dead.

Suddenly I remembered that Dod Ethan had said "we" crucified Him. I looked into Dod Ethan's sorrowful brown eyes, and couldn't imagine such a thing being true. *No,*

Dod Ethan could never have done a horrible thing like that to anyone, much less Jesus. It's just not true.

I had seen Savta's eyes fly open when she heard Dod Ethan's news. Now she lay stiff as if she didn't dare move.

Then I heard sobbing. *Oh, no, Eema is crying because Jesus is dead.* I remembered Jesus gazing into my eyes, His eyes warm with love, and a great aching lump filled my throat.

Abba, beside me, protested, "Ethan, that can't be true."

"I saw it, Jonathan," he said, then bowed his head and said softly, "I saw it."

"How, Ethan? When? And, why?"

In a low quavering voice, Dod Ethan began telling us that not long ago he was appointed to sit on the Sanhedrin, our religious court of seventy-one men. The most influential Jews in Jerusalem were chosen for this honor. However, tonight my dod didn't sound proud of this. Rather, he sighed and wearily continued.

"Right before the Passover feast last week, the High Priest had Jesus arrested after dark in the Garden of Gethsemane. They'd paid one of His disciples a bag of money to lead them to Him. We on the Sanhedrin were assembled that night to try Him."

Dod Ethan's voice got louder then. He clenched his fists and peered into Abba's eyes. "The trial was rigged against Him, Jonathan. The High Priest knew He wouldn't deny He was the Son of God—and when He wouldn't deny it, we distinguished unbelievers could 'justifiably' accuse Him of blasphemy. It happened exactly that way. Then we sent Him to Pilate the Roman governor, whom we bullied into crucifying Him."

Then he almost sobbed out, "He didn't try to get loose, Jonathan! He let us crucify Him! I saw Him dying on the Cross, and you know what He said? 'Father, forgive them, for they know not what they do.'"

Abba let out a long raggedy sigh.

Through my shock, I watched Savta place her mothering hand on Abba's shoulder.

Abba reached over and took my limp hand in his. I questioned him with my eyes. *Is Jesus really dead, Abba? Why?* He just shook his head.

Then I stared down at the mat and my thoughts went tumbling again. *Why would they crucify our Messiah?* A picture of them nailing wonderful Jesus to a Cross began forming in my mind. I shook it out of my head.

I won't believe it … no, this can't be. How I wanted it not to be true. *But Dod Ethan has never lied to me … it must be true. Oh, Jesus … did you die?*

The room didn't seem so lovely to me now. I wanted to cry out, "Dod Ethan, how could you have agreed to kill my Jesus?"

Dod Ethan's low voice interrupted my tangled thoughts. He said, "Listen to me, Jonathan."

Then the sound of Eema's soft weeping from her corner was the only sound in the room. "Oh … oh …" I stared dully at the wall over Savta's bed.

Suddenly Dod Ethan spoke again, louder. "Listen to me, Jonathan."

When Abba turned his perplexed face toward him, Dod spoke his words very deliberately. "That's not all of it, Jonathan … there's more …" He swallowed hard, then said, "He …

apparently … has risen from the dead."

"What?" Abba said like a man awakening. "What did you say?"

I saw Savta remove her hand from Abba's shoulder and close her eyes again.

"Yes, they say He's been seen right outside His tomb," Dod Ethan said, "and many other places around the city," motioning with his hands, "in Bethany and," then he shuddered, "even here in Galilee. Some have seen the nail prints in His hands."

"He's alive again?" Abba said, coming up on his knees and grabbing Dod Ethan by the shoulders to look deeply into his eyes. "Is that what you said, Ethan? Is that what you said?" When he saw the answer, he looked over Dod Ethan's head at Eema. Their eyes locked, and I watched the sorrow melt out of them.

Eema spoke in a dazed voice, "Jonathan, He died, but He's alive again." She lifted her head and cried, "Yes Jesus! you are the Son of God!"

And Abba threw his arms up in the air and shouted, "Yes, you are!"

But then Dod Ethan said shakily, "Yes, Jonathan. Now, what should *I* do?" His shoulders always held straight and strong were bowed, and his beard lay crumpled on his chest. "I am convinced that I have been instrumental in crucifying the Son of God. What should I do? I know He has risen from the dead, too. I am afraid. What should I do?"

Savta rose up from her pillows and looked at Dod Ethan. "Wait a minute, son. You don't have to believe that! For all you know that man is a fake, or even of the devil. If so, He *was* a blasphemer."

"I don't know ... I just don't know." Dod kept his eyes on the mat beneath him. He wouldn't look at Abba or me.

I guess no one felt like saying anything after that—it was quiet for several minutes. Still stunned, I just closed my eyes. Then I heard Abba shifting his weight. When I looked, I saw him reaching his hand over to Dod's bowed shoulder. Then Dod lifted his guilt-ridden eyes to Abba's.

"Ethan, we have endured a great shock this evening, and you, too, have gone through a terrible ordeal." Abba removed his hand from his shoulder and gently took Dod's hand in his. "But, there is a feeling in my heart that all will be well for you, as it is for us. We will have our supper, and then we will talk more, my brother." He smiled into his sad brown eyes and said, "The Son of God forgave you and asked His Father to forgive you, didn't you say? Perhaps you should believe that you are forgiven."

Then Abba rose up, and said with a relieved smile, "Cilla, isn't it time we eat? We have talked enough. Didn't you say you were making a pot of delicious beans and some of my favorite cinnamon-flavored bread for supper? If it's ready, let's eat it now. I'm hungry."

I got up and helped Eema arrange the food so everyone could reach it. Abba held my and Savta's hands and thanked the Lord for our food, ending his thanks with some new special words, *In the name of Jesus, Amen.*

After supper, Abba and Dod Ethan went outside to feed the animals. When Eema started gathering up the dishes, I knew it was my job to help Savta dress for bed. Though I'd often felt unappreciated by Savta, I had never really felt *angry* with her before. She believed Jesus was a blasphemer, a fake, and of the devil. She was probably glad they crucified Him!

Savta watched my face as I helped her into her nightgown. I felt numb and didn't want to talk even if I knew what to say. After I brushed her hair, I bent down and kissed her forehead. Her eyes followed me as I straightened up. I tried to smile, but it didn't work. The best I could do was say, "Good night, Savta," as Eema and I prepared to leave.

I looked back at her reclining on her pillows, noticing her pinched and tired expression. With unhappy eyes, she said softly, "Good night, Lanee."

Oh, Savta, they crucified Him! I wished I could run to her lap and bury my face in it. But, no, she didn't believe in Jesus, so I couldn't. I followed Eema out and shut the door behind us.

Abba and Dod Ethan were standing in front of Savta's door deep in conversation. We knew they were discussing Jesus, so we kissed Abba and headed home alone.

It was a dark, balmy night. Soon the rain would come. *My mind is like those lowering clouds above us. So heavy—about ready to burst.*

Plodding down the dark road, I broke the silence. "Why did Jesus have to die? And why did He have to die and then rise again?" My throat ached with the lump that was still there. "He was helping us feel like God was right here with us. So, why couldn't He have just gone on doing that?"

Walking close enough to rub arms, Eema answered, "I don't know, Lanee. But I rejoice that He is alive again."

I felt desperate. "Dod Ethan said some have seen the nail prints in His hands. I want to go find Him, Eema," I said.

"Where would we go? We can't do that." Her voice grew

calm as she said, "We will trust Him to help us to know what to do now."

We walked on in the quiet. Only halfway there, I yawned and whimpered, "Oh, Eema, I am so tired."

She slipped her arm around my waist, and I leaned on her the rest of the way home.

In the night, I heard the hard rain pounding on my roof. Reaching out to Him hopelessly, I prayed, "Oh, Jesus, if I could only see you again."

Then I cried.

CHAPTER FIVE

BEN!

JESUS was all everyone talked about in Arbela the next week. Though the news was that Jesus both died and arose, a rumor circulated that Jesus' body had been stolen by his disciples to only make it look like He'd come back to life. That was what everyone but us few seemed to believe.

Sarah greeted me as soon as I stepped into the door of the synagogue, "Well, Lanee, have you seen your precious 'Messiah' since He 'rose from the dead'?"

I was glad I'd already done my crying. I answered, "No, Sarah, but I wish I could." *Oh, how I wish I could!*

She laughed and walked off. Sarah was one important person—the apple of her abba's eye. She even looked like our rabbi. Her hair was as red as the sorrel stallion Yosef kept in his stables. Her nose was sprinkled with freckles that matched her hair. It was a pretty combination actually, but her mean ways made her seem ugly to me. *Why does she hate Jesus so? I guess she never got to smile into His eyes like I did. Oh, Jesus.*

The talk about Jesus died down some as the day approached for the feast. It was the end of the barley harvest, and Yosef always hosted a banquet at the inn to celebrate his bountiful crop. He invited the whole village to a feast of fish, fowl, vegetables, fresh fruits, and bread made from the harvested barley. I'd heard from the other girls, who'd heard it from their brothers that Ben was coming. Would I get to talk to him?

We were making new clothes for the feast. Eema and I had finished spinning our flax, and she'd woven the thread into beautiful linen cloth. We sun-bleached some of it to the palest gold. Then she stitched me a soft flowing tunic and a matching girdle out of it. I began hemming and embroidering another square of the cloth for an elegant headscarf. Maybe I would embroider the girdle, too. The calfskin sandals that Dod Ethan brought went just right with my new clothes.

Abba gave me a compliment at supper last week. He said I looked beautiful since the summer sun had tanned my face to the color of toasted almonds. I thought that at least I might look *delicious.* Sometimes Eema combed my hair as she did when I was little. Yesterday as she stood behind me combing, she said admiringly, "You should see how the sun has kissed your hair with its golden rays, Lanee." If only I were as pretty as they made me feel!

I worked every day embroidering the trailing grapevine over my headscarf and girdle. The vine, tiny leaves, and little bunches of miniature grapes here and there gradually grew around the edge of my headscarf. I liked needlework, but this was taking a long time. When I returned from helping Savta in the afternoon, I took my work out to the courtyard and got busy.

The best place was at Abba's wooden table under the shady oak tree. Sewing in the afternoon quiet with only the *er-er-erking* of chickens scratching around comforted me. As I pulled on the needle I thought about Jesus—the sound of His voice, the look in His eyes. I recalled the blessing He gave me with the little children. How would I keep my promise to tell others about Him?

I sadly mused, *"The good shepherd giveth his life for the sheep?* I remembered how scared I'd felt when He said it. Now it had happened. *But why did you have to die, Jesus?*

I tried to imagine how it would feel to die on a cross. I couldn't. When I began to imagine Jesus dying on one, I quickly shook it out of my head. Before Dod Ethan left, I thought about asking him to tell me about it. But I knew how wounded he was for his part in crucifying Jesus, so I didn't bring it up to him. And I wasn't sure I wanted to know how it really was.

Even though my dod heard Abba suggest that Jesus had forgiven him, his eyes were still full of grief the last time I saw him. He'd returned to Jerusalem to get my aunt and cousins then he planned to come back to Savta's for a vacation from the city.

What was Jesus like now that He had been dead? Would He look like a ghost? I really wanted to see Him again, but I might as well admit it, I'd be afraid to. *Oh, my Messiah, where are you? Are You different now? Jesus, I love you. Do you hear me? Why did you have to die?*

Impatient with the quiet being my only answer, I dropped my embroidering and ran up the stairs to the rooftop. Up there I felt the breeze that was stirring the highest leaves of the oak tree. Wrapping my arms around the parapet, I rested my head on the cool plaster. Thoughts of Ben tiptoed into my mind.

I remembered the first time I saw him. I was at the well early that day, so I was alone. I'd just finished filling my jug to the brim when a group of noisy boys came jostling each other down the street. The leader was a boy I'd never met. Ours is a small Jewish village where everyone knows everyone else, so who was this boy?

With his head held high and a thatch of dark hair falling over his forehead, he was headed in my direction. I saw him lift his hand and sweep his unruly hair back out of his eyes. That was both funny and appealing to me. I stared as the boys came closer. They must have been going to the synagogue, maybe for Hebrew lessons.

The new boy was doing all the talking. He was walking between Matthew and Simon, Misha's brothers, who both were grinning at him. When he swung his head from Matthew to Simon, he caught sight of me. I *was* staring at him. He kept talking to them and looking at me. I didn't stop staring. (I'm not usually so bold around boys, but this time I just couldn't drop my eyes.) They drew closer to me at the well, and he steadily gazed at me with those beautiful dark eyes.

Then I could hear what he was saying. "That donkey gave out a 'hee-haw!' and started bucking like a wild stallion! My abba was taken by surprise ..." With one passing flash of his dark eyes, he walked past me. I listened as they walked on, "But Abba held on and rode the wild thing!" That made all the boys burst out laughing.

That's when I came to myself. Well, not quite. Before, I was myself. Now, I was ... different. I felt supremely happy, and also I felt a little ashamed. Could a twelve-year-old fall in love? With a boy she didn't even know?

Soon I learned his name. Misha found it out from her brothers—Benjamin ben Jacob. He's eighteen now. His family had just moved here when I saw him that first day.

Even though he stared back at me by the well, he's never paid me any attention since. I've seen him at our Sabbath services, but mostly he stays with his abba or talks to the other boys. Once I walked near him, looked into his eyes, and said, "Good morning." He nodded back, and that was it. I've even begun to fear that all he was thinking that day was *Why's that little girl staring at me?*

Oh, Jesus, why do I love Benjamin ben Jacob? Will he notice me at the feast? Will I get a chance to really talk to him?

I straightened up from my daydreams and hurried back down to finish my headscarf.

~~~

"Jonathan, look at Lanee in her new clothes!" The feast day had finally arrived, and I had just come down from my room.

I reached out, touched her silky hair, and said, "How nice you look too, Eema,"

She and I usually tie our hair up so we can work unhindered by it, but for this special occasion we both wore our hair down, hers falling in clean honey-colored curls almost to the backs of her knees, and mine ending a little below my waist. Eema's new tunic was a lovely pink with a headscarf to match.

Abba in his freshly made linen tunic and dark Sabbath robe said, "You two will be the prettiest at the feast."

Hoping our clothes wouldn't get too sweaty before the celebration, we took the shady shortcut through the trees instead of the sunny main road to the inn. Abba was going early to help Yosef with the food and the last minute preparations. Eema was in charge of decorating the Window Room. I was her assistant.

The first thing I did when I arrived was put on a large

apron over my new clothes. Then I tied up my hair. Out in the Yafe Perach I began to gather roses for the tables. I especially wanted the dazzling yellow ones. They were the sweetest smelling roses Yosef had. I cut red and pink blooms from the low bushes then brought a stool from the dining room. I wanted to reach the prettiest roses at the top of the tall yellow rosebush. The bush bristled with long sharp thorns.

I climbed up on the stool, reaching up as high as I could, and clipping off a beautiful cluster of yellow blooms. Holding them in my other hand, I leaned more and reached out farther for the finest ones I saw. *If I can just reach these, I'll get down and finish with the lower ones ... only a little farther ... Whoa! Help me, Jesus; I'm falling into the thorns!*

And miraculously, I stopped. *Oh, thank you, Jesus.* Then I felt two strong hands encircling my waist. Real flesh hands. That's when I knew it wasn't quite so miraculous. Whoever it was righted my balance and let go.

A male voice said, "You need to get down from there, Lanee."

I felt shaken by the near fall. Somehow, I had managed to hold on to the shears and the cluster of flowers. Clutching those, I carefully turned around on my perch to see who had caught me. And who was telling me to get down. The first thing I saw was bushy black hair falling over dark eyes. It was Benjamin ben Jacob peering up at me.

His eyes became stern and he said, "You almost skewered yourself on that rosebush and you could have stabbed yourself with those shears as you fell. If you'll step down I'll get those roses for you."

What? My face went hot. Up on that stool with his eyes only a little below mine, (I'd dreamed of such closeness hundreds of times) I forgot how dear I thought he was. My thoughts were more like, *I've made a fool of myself, and he's bossing me around!*

He took the roses from my one hand and the shears from the other, laid them down on the stone bench, then held out his hand to help me down.

Once on the ground, I said, "Uh, thank you, Benjamin. It's all right. I won't lean out like that again. I'll just cut these roses growing on the lower branches." My voice was tight with embarrassment and anger.

"Yosef sent me to help you."

"Yosef?"

"Yes, he hired me to help him during the feast."

I tried to swallow my anger as Ben picked up the shears and stepped up on the stool. He began cutting the prettiest branches, easily reaching even the farthest ones.

"Why don't you go in and get a tray to carry them so you don't get stuck?"

I looked over at the pile of roses I'd gathered on the bench nearby. Why hadn't I thought of that? *Little Lanee obeyed.*

I came back with the tray and stood down below, receiving the beautiful flowers. I was still mad. When *he* decided we had enough flowers, he jumped down, took the tray from my hands, and carried it into the dining room. I followed him. He set the flowers down and went through the kitchen door without even a glance back at me.

Why did I ever think I liked that boy? I jerkily began arranging the flowers in the clay pots for the center of the tables. *"If you'll step down, I'll get those roses for you,"* Oh! *That's the part I couldn't stand!*

47

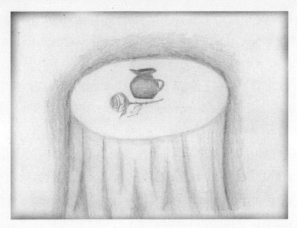

I tried to calm down. But each beautiful rose I picked up reminded me of the whole incident. *Oh, my, Jesus, why did it have to be like this?*

Uh … wait a minute. Like a lamp being lit, I suddenly realized I had been speaking to Jesus in my mind! *Why am I doing that?*

I'd been speaking to Him just as if He could hear me. *I must think He is listening.*

Is He? Jesus, have you heard me talking to you in my mind? I knew I was doing it again, but it was the only way I knew to communicate with Him. *Is it all right to think you're listening? Are you listening?*

Standing at the table draped with its linen cloth, a cluster of yellow roses poised in my right hand, I felt my mind fly away to our grassy field. There His eyes were shining down on mine. Again, I sensed, *He loves me.*

The next moment I placed the cluster of roses into the pot knowing He'd heard me. I said softly, "Thank you, Jesus."

Then I noticed the pretty roses weren't bathed in my embarrassment anymore. Somehow, Jesus had cooled my anger, and given my heart ease from the encounter with Ben. Once more, I whispered, "Oh, thank you, Lord."

Soon the decorating was finished, and everyone began to arrive for the feast. It was one of the great yearly events in Arbela. The traveling band Yosef hired to entertain us had made it. The three of them were over by the window setting up their instruments. Their costumes were festive—the men wore purple and white striped tunics girded at the waist with shiny black leather. Scarlet hats dipped down over one eye. The woman's robe was a gorgeous green, belted with a bright orange sash. She wore her long brown hair parted in the middle and draping over her shoulders. When the handsome gray-haired man began picking a lively tune on his polished lute, the woman placed the pipe to her lips and joined him. With a chuckle, the large bearded young man with dancing eyes began tapping the lively rhythm on his barrel drum. The feast had begun!

The first thing all of us girls did was admire each other's new clothes. Though I was complimented for my embroidered headscarf and girdle, I saw that Abba was wrong about me being the prettiest. Surely, Deborah was! Her garment was made of costly black silk set off by an ornate girdle of many colors. The same bright fabric held her soft black curls back from her forehead. How beautiful she was!

It didn't matter so much to me that I wasn't the prettiest, for I had decided to ignore Ben. Jesus had removed the angry feeling, but after what happened, it seemed foolish to think he could be interested in me.

As usual, Abba and our family sat at Yosef's table. We all bowed our heads as Yosef thanked the Lord for the great harvest of grain, then we began feasting on the luscious meal. I tapped my foot when the band played my favorite, *Old Nathaniel and Little Peep.*

At first, Ben stood behind Yosef's chair until he was excused to sit with his family. I saw his abba nodding and his eema smiling proudly at him. I made myself look in a different direction.

Rabbi ben Tzadik and his family sat at the other head table with several of the town's most prestigious men and their families, Deborah and Sarah included. Tonight it seemed that the rift about Jesus was forgotten—everyone wanted to enjoy the inn, the good food, and the sweet music.

Though I didn't care, I saw Ben was everywhere during the feast. Before the meal, I'd heard Yosef send him out to help with the livestock and wagons. He'd come back, and Yosef had given him the job of pouring water over the guests' feet to wash off the dust, and offering them towels to dry them. When we ate, he helped Abba serve the meat and carried tankards of drinks from the kitchen. Yosef called on him during the meal to go back to the kitchen for more fish, more watermelon, and more bread. He seemed to be enjoying his role as both server and guest.

When it was time for dessert, a tan wrist nearly covered by a white linen sleeve reached for my empty cup. I glanced up into the dark eyes of the one who didn't matter, and said softly, "Thank you." My heart beat a little faster when I saw a small smile curve his lips. He passed on to Eema's cup. I felt confused. *Do I like him, or not?*

After the meal, all of us young people were sent out to the Yafe Perach to play games while the adults visited. Everyone wanted to play a game called "Oh, Where Are You?" We'd all played this game a thousand times, but it was more fun than any other. As usual, one of us girls had to be the hunter, so I volunteered. I turned my back to the court as everyone else ran to hide. *I guess Ben is still inside clearing tables.* I waited. *He smiled at me.* I couldn't hear anymore shuffling of feet. *Now!*

I whirled around hoping to catch someone slow to hide, calling out "Oh, where are you?" That would be the quickest way to win. They'd be caught without a slap.

Everything was absolutely still. I got up and stepped cautiously away from the bench, on high alert for a hider. As I reached the middle of the court, I heard racing feet. Too late, I felt several hands slap my shoulder from behind. Laughter erupted along with, "Here I am!"

I thought I saw some movement under the low-hanging mulberry branches. I eased toward it and suddenly spied Elisabeth. She tried to jump up and tag me but wasn't quick enough. I gave her arm a quick slap and cried, "There you are!"

Everyone else came out of hiding, and it was Elisabeth's turn to hunt. I scurried to hide in the stable. When I peered back around the corner, I saw someone else running toward my hiding place. He sprinted fast and hard, for surely Elisabeth would turn. As he ran, he laughed. It was Ben! He was still wearing his apron that flapped around his churning legs. I quit looking and flattened out against the wall. The next moment he rounded the corner and plowed into me.

Again, he caught me to keep me from falling. This time, he didn't let go right away.

When he did, he turned to sneak another look from

behind the wall. Still laughing, he whispered, "Shh. She's close! Wait." He peeked out again. "She's going the other way. Now, Lanee!"

He grabbed my hand and pulled me over the court faster than I'd ever run. Elisabeth cried out and gave chase. Usually this is the best part of the game. But this time I couldn't keep up, and he had to drag me along. Elisabeth's long legs brought her closer every second. How were we going to avoid her slap and get our own in? The others left their hiding places and ran to tag her, crying out, "Here I am!"

Ben pulled me with him as he twisted and doubled back. Suddenly Elisabeth turned from chasing us and slapped Daniel on the wrist, yelling, "There you are!" Sweet words! Just to be safe we both gave her a slap and cried, "Here I am!" We had escaped.

I was out of breath. Gasping, I peeked over at Ben. His face was red from running too. "Sorry, Daniel, she was just too fast for you!" he said, laughing.

"I know you're glad, for she just about had you two!" Daniel crowed back.

"Yes, thanks friend, I'll return the favor sometime." And we all laughed.

He hasn't let go of my hand. I wiggled my hand a little in his, and he took a better hold.

Daniel sat down on the bench, and everyone ran to hide. But Ben led me toward the inn's corner. We passed through the opening between the rooms and out around the inn to the shore of the lake.

The moon was bright, and I moved through its light as

if I were dreaming. A breeze coming in from the water lifted my hair off my neck and cooled it. All I could think of was my fingers intertwined in Ben's fingers. Never having held any boy's hand, I didn't know what to do.

We walked up to the lake's edge in the moonlight. We stood that way for a time. Our friends began yelling behind us. Their voices echoed over the quiet dark lake.

Then I felt him catch my other hand in his, and pull me around to him. His face, the dear face I *had* dreamed of for many months, was very close to mine. In the moonlight, I saw that he had long lashes, and that his short beard seemed soft the way it hugged his firm jaw.

Suddenly the courtyard noise quieted. The new hush revealed frog songs all around us.

I couldn't imagine what was going to happen next. He looked into my eyes, and I saw his settle down from excited-with-laughter to serious-with-interest to there-you-are, as he looked at me when I was twelve.

"Lanee …"

I felt his strong hands slightly squeezing mine, as if he was still excited.

His dark eyes held mine. Then he lifted his to the stars over my head and said, "What did you think of Jesus?"

He lowered his gaze back to mine for the answer. Surprise sprang up in my heart and surely into my eyes too. It was at once the best thing that had ever happened to me.

"I love Him, Ben," I said softly.

The look he gave me then was the same one Abba gave me when I said Jesus would make a wonderful Son of God.

It searched me.

"Benjamin ben Jacob! Will you come?" It was Yosef.

CHAPTER SIX

JESUS IS GONE

THE rooftop beside my room was just the refuge I needed. I couldn't sleep after such an amazing night. *Did Ben really hold my hand?* I pulled the sheet up tighter around my shoulders against the cool night air.

Jesus, I know you hear me now. I want to tell you the best part of the wondrous night was when you showed me again that you love me. I don't know where you are or what you're like now, but somehow I know you're also here with me. Did you have to die for this to happen? I wish I could understand.

I gazed out into the black night. Millions of stars glistened in their lovely black setting. I leaned out over the parapet and saw the Lord's dipper pouring out over my house. Surely, I was receiving His blessings.

Suddenly a desire to speak to my God sprang up inside of me. *God in Heaven, your Son is helping me so! He knows me! He loves me! Lord God, thank you for Jesus!*

Joy bubbled up in me and I shouted, "Hallelujah!"

I heard it echo back at me from the dark hills.

Oh! What if I woke up Eema and Abba? Well … I'll just have to tell them I couldn't help it.

The quiet came back, folded its arms around me, and brought sweet thoughts of Ben. *He came to me. He chose me. Unbelievable!*

When we heard Yosef's call out by the lake, we walked

back around to the brightly lit Window Room. Yosef smiled when he saw us and said, "Benjamin, please help the stable hand. The guests are leaving now."

Ben nodded and left my side for the outer court. I could hear Eema and Abba talking in the kitchen. The sound of crockery against crockery told me they were washing the dishes. I saw the band was packing up their instruments. Yosef and I started gathering up flowerpots and removing the soiled tablecloths to get things ready for the next morning's breakfast customers. Looking elegant in his richly embroidered party robe, Yosef hummed a tune the band had played while we rearranged the tables. Ben returned, saying all the guests were gone.

Yosef, seeming satisfied that the cleanup was done, said, "Lanee, you and Benjamin come with me."

We followed him to his room. He sat down at his ancient desk and opened a side drawer. Pulling out two silver coins, he handed me one and Ben one. "Here is your pay, for you did a fine job tonight."

Surprised, I said, "No, Yosef. You didn't hire me. I was helping tonight like I always do."

He waved his hand, dismissing my argument, "Yes, you have always helped; but tonight I want to give you a reward for your work. All right, Little One?"

His watery eyes were pleasantly smiling up at me. I sensed he was proud of me. So, happily I said, "Thank you, Yosef."

Ben and I left his office and walked across the flower courtyard. He caught my hand in his near the doorway of the Window Room. The fragrance of the roses nearby, the light in Ben's eyes, and the curving of his lips into a tender smile

56

all melt together in my mind as the sweetest of memories. He said, "I'll see you again this Sabbath. Can we talk after the service?"

I told him with a happy smile, "Yes, I would like that, Ben."

Just then, Eema and Abba came out ready to start home. I followed them as they enjoyed their feast all over again—the food, the music, everyone's new clothes, what this one said to that one. Behind them, I thought, *How did a night that began so terribly, end up so beautifully?* They walked and talked, as I floated home on a cloud.

I'm still floating, Lord. Nestling deeper inside the sheet, I turned my face toward the grassy field where I first met Jesus. How surprised I was when Ben asked me what I thought of Him. Could I ever tell it all? I wonder what *he* thought of Jesus. *That's something I'll ask him this Sabbath.*

Sleepy at last, I went through the doorway to my cozy mat and snuggled in.

~~~

The summer morning sunbeam was working its way up from my feet, and I was trying my best to ignore it. It woke me again prying my eyelids open. I heard voices downstairs.

Curious, I got up and dressed, then ran down the stone stairs barefoot. Dod Micah, Eema's long and lean baby brother, was standing in the doorway between the court and the house. He had his arms raised, bracing himself against the lintel, chatting with Eema. She was outside in the court. I almost laughed aloud when I saw it was my favorite uncle. Dod Micah was about thirty years old and not yet married (I pity his poor wife when he does!)

Suddenly I realized he was standing in a wonderfully

vulnerable position. I just couldn't miss such an opportunity. I sneaked up behind him and got him in the most ticklish spot of the whole human body—the armpits! You should have seen him jerk down his arms. He whipped around in surprise.

"Lanee! You didn't tickle me? Young lady, you're in big trouble!" I ran away, but he caught me in the front room and tickled me unmercifully. When he saw Eema standing in the doorway laughing, he ran over and tickled her all around the neck and ears. She can't stand that, and he knew it. I hurried out to rescue her, tickling him off her. Eema fought back too, getting him good in the ribs.

"Stop, stop, two against one," Dod Micah gasped, "I give up."

"Serves you right, Micah," was Eema's laughing reply. "How many tricks have you played on my poor Lanee?"

"And who taught me all those tricks?" he countered, and then turned his merry face toward me. "Lanee, you're really blessed. You should have been the baby boy in a house full of older sisters!"

Eema's laughter turned into a sweet smile as she looked into her brother's slim face for a long moment. "Yes, I remember the day you were born, Micah. How blessed we felt."

Eema picked up a jug of pomegranate juice, and said, "Lanee, bring the cups into the front room." She led us into the cool shady room, and began pouring the spicy red juice into a cup for Dod.

"When did you come, Dod, and how long can you stay?" I asked as we all sat down with our drinks. We always had the best times when Dod Micah came. He lived in Bethany, a village near Jerusalem. "Will you stay with us?"

"Well, before I was so discourteously interrupted by a certain tickling girlie-girl, I was telling your eema that I'm on my way to Damascus." Then I saw mischief steal across his face. "Guess what, Lanee? *I've* fallen in love! And wouldn't you like to know with whom?"

That got me laughing again. "Oh no, Dod Micah. Does she know how you really are, and what she'll have to endure if she marries you?"

He pretended to be offended and said, "The one I love knows all about me, and still loves me dearly."

I hate to admit it, but he'd made me really curious. I looked over at Eema who smiled mysteriously at Dod Micah's words. "Do you know who it is, Eema?"

Eema shook her head at her brother and said, "Yes, it is the one we were talking about when you came downstairs."

Dod Micah's lips were pressed together and his eyes were dancing. He lifted his eyebrows, inviting me to give up.

"Oh, Dod Micah, I can't guess! Please just tell me!"

He set his cup down, got up from the soft brown cushions, and came to me. Pulling me up from my seat into his slender arms, he said with merriment in his voice, "It's Jesus, Lanee. It's Jesus! He is my Savior!"

Then Dod Micah held me in his sweet hug. I could hear his heart beating against my temple. I thought, *He called you his "Savior." I've never heard anyone call you that.* In a moment, I felt Eema's arms circle us both.

"Do you know that we love Him too, Dod?" I spoke up out of the cozy cocoon. "We met Him right here in the fields behind our house."

Eema and Dod Micah let go, and he smiled down at me. "Your eema told me so, Lanee, but I'm glad you love Him enough to say it. Many are afraid to in Jerusalem." He retrieved his cup and went to the open doorway to look out on the morning. "Jesus spent many days in Bethany near my house. My neighbors, Mary and Martha, were close friends of His." He turned around and asked Eema, "Did you know He raised their brother Lazarus from the dead?"

We both cried, "He did?"

Then she said, "Oh my, we haven't heard that, Micah. Please tell us about it."

"I saw Jesus call him out of his tomb. It was a mighty miracle. But the most magnificent deed I witnessed was Jesus being crucified, Cilla. How brave He was! Every time I look at my own hands I remember those horrible nails in His."

He paused and studied his hands for a moment, then went on. "He had to push himself up on the spike they nailed through His feet to exhale and to take each new breath. I wanted to run away and not watch it, but I couldn't leave. I felt like He wanted me to stay until the end." Dod's eyes were far away. "I was there when the rich man, Joseph of Arimathaea, took His body to his own new tomb not far from where He was crucified. Even though it was the saddest day I ever lived, I always get excited when I talk about it!" He began walking up and down in the room. "How He loves us! How He suffered! What He was willing to go through for us!"

I stood up in his path and said, "Why, Dod? Why *did* He have to die?" Hot tears blurred my vision.

He stopped. Taking my shoulders into his slim hands, he

said, "Lanee, He had to die to shed His blood. We needed it."

"We did? More than we needed Jesus to be with us?" That's when my tears really flowed over.

"Yes, much more," he said kindly. "You see, Lanee, the Scriptures say the only way sin can be paid for is by blood being shed. The whole human race needed Jesus to shed His blood to pay for our sins."

Searching his deep brown eyes, I shook my head and said, "I don't understand, Dod Micah."

He let go of my shoulders and said, "Let's sit down, and I'll try to explain it to you." My fun-loving uncle, who was usually never serious with me, sat with his chin in his hand, thinking.

"It began with Adam and Eve in the Garden of Eden. They did the one thing God said not to do—they ate the forbidden fruit. It was the first sin. Their eyes flew open to evil, showing them their nakedness before our holy God and before each other. God had to slay sinless animals to make coats to cover their nakedness. You remember all that don't you, Lanee?"

I nodded.

"Then they found out the true horror of sin. It separated them from God! No longer could they talk with Him in the cool of the day. Their sin had destroyed that fellowship. And, not only were *they* separated from God, but all their offspring were, too.

"He didn't want to be separated from His creation, so God, through Abraham, Isaac, and Jacob, chose the Jews to draw near to himself." He smiled and said, "Thank God. Remember, Lanee, we were slaves in Egypt, but God sent word to Pharaoh to let us go. Pharaoh wouldn't do it, so God sent plagues to the Egyptians."

Dod Micah got up and paced over the floor as he talked, his hands clasped behind him, "This is the part I wanted to get to. The death angel was sent to slay the Egyptians' first-born sons. God told Moses to tell our forefathers to brush the blood of a spotless lamb on the doorposts and the lintels of their houses. Because of its covering, all the Jews' houses were passed over by the death angel. The lambs died, so our first-born could go on living. From then on, God has allowed a substitute to take the punishment for our sins." Dod Micah stopped in front of me. "Do you know what the punishment for sin is, Lanee?"

"God told Adam the day he ate the forbidden fruit he would die. It's death, isn't it, Dod?"

"Yes, it is. Every evening and morning, a lamb dies in our Temple, besides many other animals as substitutes for the punishment for our sins. The poor animals' lives are sacrificed to *clear* us from sin in God's sight. But, Lanee, the lambs' blood could not *cleanse* us from the sin. Our hearts, minds, and souls were still polluted by the influence of sin. Adam wore the coat, but he was still separated from God."

Dod Micah sat back down and looked at the two of us, the sadness he talked of written across his lean face. What he'd said was plain—we were lost away from God and couldn't do anything about it. Feeling how tragic it really was, I slumped down on my stool.

"But don't despair, Lanee, God wasn't satisfied to leave us there with no hope of ever getting back together with Him. Our great Lord God sent His own Son, Jesus Christ, to this world. His plan would completely do away with sin, its effects, and even our sinful nature that plagues us. John the Baptist pointed to Jesus and said, 'Behold the Lamb of God, which takes away the sin of the world.'"

Suddenly I knew where he was going. "Do you mean God sent Jesus to die instead of the lambs?" I asked, astonished.

Dod cried, "That's exactly it, Lanee! He came to be my substitute. He came to take my punishment." Tears filled Dod Micah's eyes. "He came to shed His blood so my sins could be washed away in it, to cleanse my heart from the effects of sin, and to wash my very inner nature of all its sinful ways. He came to bridge the separation between me and God!"

I was thunderstruck. The realization that Jesus came to die because I was unfit for God rolled over me. I felt like I did the night that we learned that He was crucified; only this time, it wasn't Dod Ethan's fault—it was *mine!*

Jesus, you had to die because of my sin—because of my separation from God. Oh, no!

Then Dod threw his head up and cried out to Jesus, "Lord, how can I ever repay you? I love you for my precious salvation, Savior!"

I was surprised when Eema suddenly closed her eyes and lifted her hands. She prayed, "Jesus, take your powerful blood and wash me like you have Micah. I desire to be clean from sin in every part of my being."

That's when I thought of the pride and anger I felt toward Ben at the feast. I knew I needed cleansing, too! "Oh, wash me, too, Lord Jesus! You bled on the Cross, so that I could be made clean like you. Please forgive me and cleanse me!" I cried through my guilty tears.

Dod Micah's passionate words continued, "When I saw

Him suffering on that Cross it seemed so senseless. I would have done anything to get Him loose from that horrible death. But He had told us it was His Father's will, so we couldn't even try to help Him. I didn't understand why God would let Jesus die like that." Dod paused, his eyes narrow and sad.

"We were so disappointed when He left us for those three days. But then He arose, Lanee! He called five hundred of us followers together at once, where He helped us understand God had sent Him to be our substitute."

"Oh, Dod, did you see the nail prints in His hands?"

"Yes, I did." Dod Micah stretched his open hands toward Eema and me. "He showed them to us and told us to go preach His death and Resurrection to the people. If they believe and repent, He will wash their sins away in His blood. I saw Him and I heard Him."

"Oh, where is He, Dod Micah? I want to see Him too!"

"He's gone, Lanee, Jesus is gone! He told us, 'Behold, I send the promise of my Father upon you: but tarry in the city of Jerusalem, until you are endued with power from on high.' Then right outside of Bethany a cloud lifted Him up out of this world!"

Eema stood up, "You mean Jesus went to Heaven?"

"Yes, He's there now!" Dod went over to her and hugged her. His face was aglow when he looked into her eyes and said, "Dear sister, Heaven is so real to me now that I know Jesus is there."

Suddenly Dod Micah remembered something. "Right now, I need to leave for Damascus to buy those supplies for the bakery. Did you know Jesus promised to send us 'another Comforter' when He got back to Heaven? Many are gathered in Jerusalem waiting, and I want to be there when He comes!" He kissed me on the cheek and turned toward the door.

But immediately he turned back, looking amazed. "Oh, Lanee, you need to be there too! Cilla, tell Jonathan, and all of you come to Jerusalem soon. He's going to send the promised Comforter any time now!"

I sought Eema's eyes. The night we learned of Jesus' crucifixion she had said, "We will trust Him to help us know what to do now." Her smile told me she understood what I did. Through the blessing of an unexpected visit of my favorite uncle, Jesus was letting us know.

CHAPTER SEVEN

GOING AFTER THE PROMISE

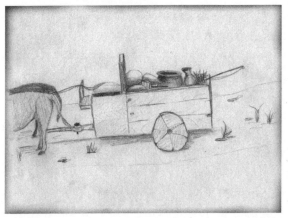

*T*O Jerusalem for the promise, the promise. He'll send us another Comforter, Comforter. To Jerusalem for the promise, the promise. The words kept time with the slap of my sandals on the hard dusty road. Had it only been two days since Dod Micah's visit? Yet we were far south of Arbela on the way to the holy city, hoping to make it in time.

Abba started planning for the trip as soon as we told him Dod Micah's news. "This coming week is the feast of Pentecost," he said. "Perhaps Yosef would like to send his offering to the Temple and will allow me to take it for him. Also I must see if Savta is well enough for us to leave."

Savta *was* better. She hadn't needed our help as much, so that might work out. Oh, how I hoped Yosef would agree for Abba to go.

When he came back that evening, he had some surprising news. First, Yosef wanted to close the inn for two weeks and make the trip with us! Could it be? And when Abba went by Savta's, he found Dod Ethan and Dodah Ruth there. They were going to visit for the next two weeks. We could go!

Traveling through Galilee was beautiful. The rolling hills were carpeted with their thick green summer grass. Oak, myrtle, and cedar trees lined the road meandering through our country's wheat fields, where hundreds of workers were busy harvesting the golden heads of grain.

Though Yosef had a ripening wheat field, he had done an unheard of thing—he'd left the harvesting to his farming partner. The morning we departed, he'd shown up driving a loaded wagon to our door. In front, two friendly-looking donkeys pulled, and the bed was a big jumble of stuff—burlap bags of grain for the Temple and buckets full of lemons, onions, pomegranates, and garlic. Up against the seat was a bundle of clothes, a large basket of food, a cask of water, and a skin of juice. A brass pot, a shovel, and an axe were piled on, and last of all a fishing pole stuck out the back gate.

He said, "Just bring your clothes. I have everything else we'll need!" It was a good thing, for how would anything else fit?

For the first miles, Yosef and I sat up in the seat of the wagon while Eema and Abba walked along beside it. I glanced over at Yosef's dark wrinkled face and smiled when he nodded at me. I was glad he came. He clicked his jaw to the donkeys and looked glad too.

"Do you like my donkeys, Lanee?"

I grinned and said that I did. Then he told me their names were Wheat and Chaff. Wheat was slick and honey-colored, and Chaff had a rough light-brown coat. I thought of the shiny grains of wheat Eema and I ground to make bread and the dry husk around the grains we let blow away in the wind called the chaff. What funny names for donkeys!

Yosef said, "Just wait, and you'll see why I named them so."

It was about noon on that first day of our journey, when suddenly Chaff sat down in the middle of the dusty road. It startled Abba who was driving the wagon. He pulled on the reins to stop Wheat from plodding on. All at once Chaff hustled up and went running back the way we'd come. He pulled Wheat and the wagon around with him. That's when Yosef hurried to the back of the wagon and grabbed a feedbag. I didn't know Yosef could move so fast! As soon as that wayward donkey heard the rattle of feed in the bag, he abruptly stopped. When he greedily lowered his head into the bag, Yosef strapped it onto him.

"I try not to let Chaff get hungry," Yosef explained, still breathing hard. "When that happens all he can think of is his stall full of sweet hay, and instantly he wants to fly away in that direction." He slipped Wheat's feedbag on and suggested we stop for our noon meal, too. That sounded good to me. The sun was beating down on our heads, and my stomach was growling. We pulled the wagon over to the shade of a large oak tree.

Yosef fed us smoked perch and soft bread, with sugary dates to top it off. How scrumptious it was after the long hot walk of the morning! I lay back on the blanket we'd spread and fell asleep. When I awoke, I heard Yosef's husky voice.

"Jonathan, I guess I'm too late to believe in Jesus now. I didn't take the time to go see Him when He was just a few miles away. Now He's gone, and I'll never have a chance. I must have been out of my mind to think the money I was making in the inn was more important than meeting the Son of God!"

I opened my eyes to just slits, still sleepy. Yosef sat on the other blanket, his leathery face grave, as he looked away across the Galilean hills. My parents were sitting on the other end of my blanket.

Abba shooed a fly off Eema's headscarf, and then said, "Is that why you came with us, Yosef?"

Yosef, instead of answering, put his face into his hands and began weeping. His old voice cracked like it wasn't often used for such a purpose. I closed my eyes and waited.

Then I heard his hoarse speech begin again. "I've not told you about my family, have I, Jonathan and Cilla?" He paused, and I heard him blow his nose. I opened my eyes enough to see him say, "My mother's people were Greeks. Her family moved to Galilee when Ptolemy reigned over us from Egypt. When my abba married her, he was the rabbi of Arbela. I was their only child.

"My abba loved the Scriptures. He could quote most of the Pentateuch, and many of the Psalms. But my eema didn't care for his religion. She thought it was strange to worship only one god, and spoke to me often of the many gods she loved. Because of my parents' different views, I was divided in my heart about what to believe.

"When my abba died, he gave me his collection of scrolls. He asked me to study them daily and pray that the Lord would help me overcome the unbelief in my heart. Eema would like to have taken them from me, so she could win me over to her beliefs, but they were all I had from my father. She couldn't do it.

"When she died, I was left alone to find my way. I have studied, yes, many years, and also I have worked. I built the inn, with your help, and began to prosper. That's when I decided it didn't matter what I believed as long as I could enjoy life and become wealthy.

"That peace ended the day I heard of Jesus. I recognized Him from the Scriptures, Jonathan! He is the Prophet that Moses said the Lord would raise up from among us. He is the 'seed of the woman' who will 'bruise the serpent's head.' I recognized Him when David said, 'The stone which the builders rejected is become the head stone of the corner.' And now that He's been crucified, I know it was Jesus that Isaiah referred to as a 'root out of a dry ground,' who would go to death 'as a lamb to the slaughter.' There are so many references to Him everywhere in the Word of the Lord. Yet, when He came so near, I would not go to Him!"

I listened to the insects buzzing around us and to Yosef weeping into his hands. Then I heard Abba. He began to pray for Yosef.

"Dearest Lord Jesus, I believe that you are God's Son. I believe that there is nothing you cannot do. Since you died on the Cross and rose again, I believe in you even more strongly. And yes, I believe you hear every prayer I pray, no matter where I am, or what I'm doing. Here we are out under this oak tree, Lord. You see my dear Yosef's tears, and you've heard his words. Will you touch his heart and let him know the joy of believing in you—the same joy you gave me and my family? I cannot help him, Lord, but I know you can! Thank you for hearing my prayer, dear Jesus."

Yosef sat with his face in his hands while Abba prayed. The moment Abba's voice stopped, Yosef's head sprang up! "Here now, what's this?" he cried. "You have touched me! You have come to *me!*" He turned to Abba, tears running down his old furrowed face, "Jonathan, Jesus has shown me I am His!"

I popped up and was amazed to see Yosef running down the road, his hands waving above his head and his robe flapping behind him. It made us all laugh aloud! *Chaff, you've met your match!*

CHAPTER EIGHT

THE PROMISE GETS SWEETER

"HAVE a drink of water, Lanee." Eema handed me the bulging skin. We were trekking down the backbone of our country on our way to Samaria, and my, was it hot! Galilee's grassy rolling hills had gradually given way to bare craggy rocks. The farther south we journeyed, the drier and rockier it was.

Yosef encouraged, "Let's press on to Samaria and then we'll rest." He knew the owner of an inn at the north entrance of the city. He was one of Yosef's distant cousins.

Yosef explained, "Demetrius' inn is much larger than mine, and is called a *caravansary*. He lodges large caravans of business travelers passing from Africa to Mesopotamia." He squinted over at Abba walking beside the wagon. "Jonathan, you may remember Demetrius. He has visited the Window Inn several times to fish in the lake. Often he has asked me to let him return the hospitality."

Yosef shook the reins and flashed the happy smile he'd had ever since Jesus spoke to him. "Tonight, if I know Demetrius, we will dine and rest in comfort."

It was late afternoon when we reached the stone wall surrounding the caravansary. Demetrius, brown and husky, came running through the gate with great joy and surprise that Yosef had come at last. He proudly offered us his best.

"Behold the wonderful deep well our caravansary is built around, Yosef. Its water is sweet and plentiful. Please leave your wagon to my servants, and come this way. You will have the finest night's rest anyone could want away from home."

We grabbed our clothes bags and followed him upstairs. Faces peeked out from behind the travelers' blankets hanging in the doorways of the downstairs rooms as we climbed the stairs. Some of the open rooms were occupied by camels, and in one, I saw a beautiful white horse.

Up the stone steps, Demetrius, robed in russet linen, took us past rooms that had doors, until we stood before an ornately carved door. With a flourish, he swung it open and said, "For you cousin Yosef, my finest suite!" It was a plush sitting room with two connected bedrooms—and just right!

"Thank you, Cousin Demetrius. We are blessed by your hospitality." Yosef gave a little bow and a big smile.

Demetrius promised to send up water so we could wash, and later he would send us some supper. We rested awhile on the soft couch and chairs until two servants came bringing large buckets of water for our baths. When Eema said I could do some exploring of the courtyard once I had bathed, I hurried through washing and dressing. I couldn't wait to see what a caravansary is all about!

Feeling clean and refreshed I descended the stairs and first peeked into the stall that held the beautiful horse. I was startled when I saw his owner in the stall grooming him. The owner was a tall, brawny Roman soldier. Quietly, I moved away.

Many travelers had come on camels. I wondered how it felt to ride a camel. How high up I would be! I stopped to watch one of the strange creatures. Where his long curved neck ended, there was the face of an old man chewing and chewing. He made me laugh.

Suddenly I saw Chaff and Wheat next door to the funny camel. We had become friends over the last few days. *How I'd love to have a donkey!* I thought, as I hurried toward them.

"Hey, girl! Girl! Watch out! Come away from there! Quick!

I turned to see who was calling, then—thump! A hard blow across my backside came from nowhere.

Ugh—face down in the dirt!

"Oh, no! I tried to warn you." Strong hands gripped me by the shoulders and pulled me up out of the dirt. "Are you hurt? Do you think you can walk? If so, we'd better move out of that camel's range!"

I let the owner of the strong hands and voice get me up and moving. When he stopped a good way off from the stable, I peered through mucky eyelashes at my rescuer.

Oh, my! It was a boy. The best-looking boy I'd ever seen! He gazed with concern into my eyes and I stared back. Only a few years older than I, dark curly hair framed a friendly handsome face, as his lovely eyes the color of a stormy sky held mine.

It's David! I thought. He was just as I had imagined our young king when I'd read about him slaying Goliath. I gaped at his beauty.

Suddenly it occurred to me that *I* was a mess! Quickly I untied my kerchief and began wiping my face.

"Uh, thank you. I think I'm all right," I said, feeling shaky from more than just the camel's kick. When he looked like he wanted to help brush the dirt off my clothes, I hurriedly began brushing them myself and said, "Oh, thank you for trying to warn me, and for pulling me out of there."

"Would you believe it ... uh ... I don't know what to call you. May I ask your name?"

"It's Lanee." I said, shyly looking up into his dusky blue eyes.

"Lanee? I've never heard that name before." He studied my face until I began to blush. "Would you believe it, Lanee, that cranky old camel almost did the same thing to me earlier? I saw him try it out of the corner of my eye and jumped to safety."

I remembered how tongue-tied I'd been with Ben and decided to press past my shyness. "Th-Thank you ... uh ... what's *your* name?"

"It's David," he said and gave me a dazzling white-toothed smile, "David, to the rescue!"

What a surprise! It is David, a now David, looking just like my prince had stepped out of the Scriptures. Only, I noticed, he wasn't really dressed like a prince. His clothes were very worn and faded.

"Let's see if you can walk, Lanee." He took my arm and walked me slowly away from the animals' stalls toward the well. "May I ask where you and your family are going? Is it to Jerusalem for the feast?"

I was glad we were taking it slow. Wincing with each step, I answered, "We're going to Jerusalem to receive the promise."

"The *promise?*" David's interest shone in his eyes.

"Yes. The promise that Jesus gave His disciples when He went up to Heaven," I said, then thought, *Maybe he doesn't even know about Jesus.*

"I knew it! I knew it! You and your family are believers, aren't you?" He turned his excited eyes fully on mine. "So are I and my mother!"

I was astonished to see David's face glowing so. How "ruddy and of a beautiful countenance and goodly to look to" he was, just as the Scriptures described our famous David.

"What did you say? Believers?" I asked.

"Yes, it's what we are being called by everyone, because we believe in Jesus Christ."

"Oh, my! Yes, we are … we do … yes … Jesus is my Savior!" I was too flustered to talk right.

David stopped walking and said, "Lanee, would you like to meet my eema? I know she'd surely like to meet you and your family."

I nodded, and he guided me to one of the small rooms off the court. An old blanket was hanging over the open doorway. David pushed aside the blanket. The tiny room was empty except for a pretty woman seated on a mat against the far wall and a small table in the center. On the table was a burlap bag.

"Eema, I want you to meet someone! Her name is Lanee. She and her family are going to Jerusalem to be there when the promise comes."

I saw her questioning look break into a bright smile. "It's a joy to make your acquaintance, daughter."

I noticed how drab her clothes were. Though it was clean, her gray tunic was worn and the headscarf she held in her lap was thin and faded.

"I'm so happy to meet you, too."

When David told her about the camel's kick, a worried look came across her face. She rose up and motioned to her mat. "Are you hurt, Lanee? Would you like to lie down?"

"At first it hurt to walk, but I'm better now," I said with a reassuring smile. "May I go tell my eema about you and ask her to visit you? She is a believer, too."

"Please do, child. I would welcome her company."

Upstairs, I found Abba in the sitting room talking over the next day's travel with Yosef, while Eema stood at the window looking out over the courtyard.

"Well, Yonina, what has happened to you to make you look so ... uh ... rosy? Abba asked.

I must have missed wiping off some of the dirt. I didn't take time to explain. "Abba, I've met some other believers— some others who love Jesus! It's a boy named David and his mother. Eema, will you come with me and visit David's mother? She is downstairs in one of the small rooms."

Eema agreed and followed me down the stairs to David's room.

"May we come in?" I called outside of the blanket. David held the blanket aside to let us in.

I could tell when Eema first saw her she liked her. She said, "Hello, I'm Priscilla, but everyone calls me Cilla."

"Welcome, Cilla. I'm Lira."

After that, David and I left them to talk while we explored the whole caravansary. We saw a large caravan with many camels entering the gate. The men who led them wore golden earrings in both ears. We heard as they called for Demetrius to take them to his best rooms. I was very glad we had arrived earlier than they.

Later we found David's mother upstairs with my family. They'd decided we would travel together the rest of the way to Jerusalem. Even though we'd just met, it felt so right that we were together. My eema told me to call David's mother, Eema Lira. And he would call my mother, Eema Cilla.

That evening I heard Eema Lira tell my eema, "When we heard the disciples were tarrying for the Lord's promise in Jerusalem, I asked the Lord to help us get there. We left our village, traveling this far by faith in Him. Now He has sent us friends to travel with the rest of the way. How I praise His name!"

Remembering that old man's face, chewing and chewing, I laughed and thought, *Thank you, Lord, for one grouchy camel!*

CHAPTER NINE

DAVID'S STORY

T HEY planned an early start, so Yosef and Abba sent us all to bed after we ate. And oh, how we ate! Demetrius sent up a delicious supper—succulent roast chicken, squash, and a spicy loaf of bread like I had never before tasted. We especially enjoyed sharing this first meal with our new friends, David and Eema Lira!

Early the next morning we loaded up the wagon and set out for Jerusalem. Our eemas rode in the wagon while everyone else walked. I really wasn't fit to sit much today due to my recent encounter with the camel.

The morning started out hot. Abba and Yosef walked up near the donkeys, with David and me following along near the wagon, or sometimes trailing behind it.

"Have you ever been on this road, David?" I asked, looking down at my old dusty sandals and trying to match his strides. I glanced over at the new friend the Lord had given me. His startling blue eyes swung around to mine, and his lips curved into a sweet smile. I beamed back at him.

"Eema and I have never traveled outside of our village before now," he said and turned back to scan the countryside. "Have you?"

"Yes, we always try to go to Passover in Jerusalem every year." *But I never had such a friend to walk along with me,* I thought, very excited about David. *Soon he'll see Jerusalem for the first time!*

Around noontime, Yosef pointed out, "There's Mount Gerizim, the Mount of Blessing, on the right, and over there to the left is Mount Ebal, the Mount of Cursing." Our road went through the valley between them. I looked at the familiar hills with new interest.

Yosef continued, "God told Moses when they went into the Promised Land to divide the tribes—half of them would stand on Mount Gerizim and half on Mount Ebal. God wanted the people to call to each other across the valley, telling whom God would bless from Mount Gerizim, and whom He would curse from Mount Ebal. Joshua did just that after he'd brought our forefathers over the Jordan River on dry land. God had Joshua build an altar of whole stones on Mount Ebal, plaster it, then write the law on its sides."

I peered through the heat at Mount Ebal. *I wonder if those stones are still there. Lord God, how real you were to Moses and Joshua. And how blessed I am that you're becoming real to me!*

Leaving the two low mountains behind, we came to a grove of date palm trees growing near the road. We stopped to eat our noon meal and rest awhile in the shade. Afterward, Yosef asked David and me to drive the wagon.

Clip clopping along the dusty road, David wanted to know all about us—where we lived, and who Yosef was to us. Then he wanted to know how we'd come to love Jesus. I told him about the days we'd heard Jesus preach, about Dod Ethan and the crucifixion, about Dod Micah coming to tell us about the promise, and even about Savta, and how she wouldn't believe in Jesus. I *didn't* tell him about Ben. *I haven't told anyone about Ben.*

"Now, it's your turn, David." I'd been wondering where

his abba was, and why he and Eema Lira dressed so poorly.

David gave me a long look and began differently than I expected.

"Do you remember back there when Yosef showed us the Mount of Cursing and the Mount of Blessing?"

I nodded.

"I know something about those mountains, Lanee, for now I've lived on both of them." David was holding the reins, his eyes toward Abba and Yosef who were walking a little ahead of the wagon. The reins rested in his two calloused hands. I'd never seen a boy's hands so work-worn.

He looked over at me and said, "Eema and I are Jews, but my father is a Roman." Watching my eyes for a moment, he turned and gazed back down the road. Then he continued, "He came through our village riding high with the other soldiers. They camped near our village, for there they could get provisions and water until their orders came to move out. My eema was sixteen years old, and surely, she was quite beautiful. My father saw her at the well one day and decided she must be his! Though I don't know how he arranged it, soon they were married.

"When it came time for the Romans to move on, he promised he would send for Eema. But, Lanee, he never has." David frowned as he combed his fingers through his dark curls. "Later I was born. We have always been alone. Eema's family has been ashamed of us—though they helped Eema to survive before I grew big enough to work. We have never belonged to *anyone*.

"All those years we lived on the Mount of Cursing, though it wasn't Mount Ebal. Eema not only felt forsaken by both my father and her father, but she also believed *God* had forsaken her, because she had married a non-Jew. She tried to find the blessings in life, but all she could do was struggle. As I grew, I couldn't grasp why I didn't have an abba like the other boys in our village. One day the boys teased me about being a Roman. When I ran home to Eema, she told me the truth.

"We were outcasts, we were poor, and we were mostly unhappy. Then Jesus came!

"I saw Him in the village one day. He was walking through the market with His disciples. I had been working for the blacksmith and had just finished for the day. Excited, I ran home to get Eema, and hurried to where Jesus was. I had longed to see Him ever since I'd heard of Him, and finally, there He was, right in front of me! My excitement calmed down to shyness.

"Our village was crowded around Him. Eema and I squeezed into a place near Him on the left. He was already speaking. 'Consider the lilies how they grow: they toil not, they spin not; and yet I say unto you, that Solomon in all his glory was not arrayed like one of these. If God so clothe the grass, which is today in the field, and tomorrow is cast into the oven, how much more will he clothe you, O you of little faith?'

"I thought, *our clothes are old and worn thin—we have no land to grow flax on. How good it would be for God to clothe us.*

"Jesus continued, 'And seek not what ye will eat, or what ye shall drink, neither be ye of doubtful mind. For all these things do the nations of the world seek after: and your Father knoweth that ye have need of these things. But rather seek ye the Kingdom of God; and all these things shall be added unto you. Fear not little flock; for it is your Father's good pleasure to give you the kingdom.'

"When He finished, He turned and looked at Eema and me! It seemed this wonderful person knew He had spoken directly to the cry of both of our hearts. Lanee, we wanted something better than the life we were living. My eema had struggled from her youth to provide for us, and we both had felt so lonely. Now Jesus was telling us with authority that God, our Father, wanted something better for us, too!

"Right there I fell down at His knees and said, 'Lord!' He laid His hand on my head, and I knew in my heart that life would never be the same. That's the day Eema and I came down off the Mount of Cursing and marched up the Mount of Blessing!"

David turned his gorgeous smile on me and said, "And that's where we are today!"

CHAPTER TEN

JERUSALEM!

Y OSEF had to recline his old bones on the blankets in the back of the wagon for the last miles. He began telling David and me stories of Arbela when he was a boy. As I walked beside David near the wagon, I realized I'd never heard any of them before. But then I'd never spent so much time with Yosef before.

A long way back, we had spotted the shining gold crown of the Temple. We were getting excited, for it still was another whole day before the feast of Pentecost. Maybe we'd arrive in time! Yosef's stories helped to pass the last hours on the road.

One of the stories was about the night the synagogue caught fire—everyone worked most of the night to put out the fire then stayed out to talk it over until morning. All the eemas went home for food, and the whole village had breakfast together. "All of us boys had the most fun we'd ever had beating out that fire!" he said laughing. After that the village had come together to build the new synagogue.

More and more dusty travelers joined us as we neared the city gate. Two boys on a donkey rode like Jehus around the slow procession whooping and waving their arms. A nearby shepherd whistled. David and I laughed when the sheep took to their hooves through the crowd with loud "baa-baas" and almost knocked him over.

As we passed through the open gate, I lifted my tired eyes to the glorious Temple, relieved that we had finally arrived. I smiled at the astonishment on David's face at his first good look at our magnificent house of God. Eema Lira spoke in wonder, "How beautiful it is!"

"Yosef, do you have any more cousins like Demetrius here in Jerusalem?" I inquired, remembering with longing the suite of rooms and the roasted chicken we enjoyed in Samaria. When it was only Abba, Eema, and I, we had always camped outside of the gates on the Mount of Olives. On this trip with Yosef, who knew what would happen?

He grinned at me and said, "No, sweet Lanee, but I believe a lake full of fish is some excellent bait to catch us a room for the night." He sat up, and noticing where we were, he directed Abba to take the right fork in the road. "I want to go toward the upper city gate, Jonathan."

A warm breeze blew across the ancient city in our direction. It carried delightful smells. I caught a whiff of roasted lamb, of something sweet with cinnamon, and of smoke from the cooking fires. Noon was a long time ago. When I remembered the soft rolls Abba brought out of the city last year to our campsite, my mouth watered.

Trying to get my mind off food, I gazed at the Temple again. It was a stunning sight, head and shoulders above every other building in Jerusalem. Its crown of golden spikes brilliantly reflected the sun's last rays. Abba said they were there to keep the birds from landing on the Temple. The afternoon sun set the huge branches of the golden vine that encircled the Temple afire. Worshipers were gathering on the marble stairs and on top of the porch roofs. The day after tomorrow was the feast of Pentecost, one of the three times in the year God's people came to worship Him in Jerusalem.

The Temple would be covered with worshipers then.

Now the road leading to the upper city was clogged with people. Family groups leading animals, wagons loaded with produce, even a wagon full of squawking chickens. Some of those walking near us were clean and nicely dressed—perhaps they were Jerusalem citizens out seeing the sights. At that moment, I envied them. How good it would be to have a bath and a comfortable place to rest for the night.

"Oh, look, Lanee. Look!" Eema cried out. Her voice sounded both sad and thrilled—like when she found Nanny Goat giving birth to her kids. I saw her suddenly break into a run up ahead of the wagon. She ran down the road and then off to the left, up a small grassless hill.

On the small hill were three stout wooden crosses.

I watched Eema run up to the center Cross and sink down. At first, I saw without comprehending. Then I remembered that Jesus died between two thieves, and I just stopped. I didn't want to go any closer.

The good shepherd will give his life for the sheep.
I willed my feet to go on. I saw other travelers look and

point, but no one else joined Eema. *Jesus died here. Jesus really died here not very long ago.*

I saw Abba pull the wagon up beside the hill. He jumped down off the seat. Yosef rolled out of the wagon bed, as David and his eema walked up beside Eema and knelt. I plodded slowly on, finally stopping at the bottom of the rocky rise. When I saw the dark stains covering the rough wood of His Cross, I felt hot tears flow over my cheeks.

He died here. Right next to the road. Everyone that passed by saw Him dying!

After a while, Abba cleared his throat and spoke. "Thank you, Lord Jesus. We thank you with all our hearts." Then he lifted Eema up, took her hand firmly in his, and they walked down to me. Gently they took my hands in theirs and walked back to the wagon. Abba helped me up into the wagon.

Jerusalem swarmed around us. We entered the gate of the upper city, where the prosperous Jews lived. Dod Ethan lived nearby. Numb, I watched Abba and Yosef leave the wagon and walk through the double doors of a bustling inn to see about rooms for us. Soon Abba returned, saying, "Yosef made his swap. I didn't think he could right here at Pentecost. The owner traded our stay for a fishing trip at the Window Inn. He even threw in the livery service for the wagon and donkeys."

It didn't matter to me anymore. I thought of His Cross and almost said aloud, *Jerusalem is a horrible place!* I was so tired and hurt, I didn't care anymore if I ate or even if I had a room or not.

I was awake when the morning broke over Jerusalem. Abba and Eema were still sleeping, and I slipped out to the rooftop. I needed a place to cry.

Why did Jesus have to die in front of everyone like He was a criminal? For the first time I pictured His suffering quite clearly. *It must have hurt you so badly to be crucified. And, oh, how you must have felt ashamed for everyone to see you bleeding and dying.*

I cried and cried. *It was for me, wasn't it, Jesus? So your blood could wash away my sin. Oh, Jesus, please forgive me for putting you through such pain. What Abba said, I feel too. Thank you, Jesus, with all of my heart. Oh, how I love you, Savior.*

When I dried my face and went back inside, Abba and Eema were up. We'd planned to go to the Temple after breakfast. I wasn't hungry, but I didn't want to worry Eema, so I ate a little. When we finished, Yosef led us out of the front door of the inn. Instead of heading toward the eastern part of the city, he retraced our path of the night before—back toward the Cross. *No Yosef, I don't want to see it again.* Even though I'd cried so, my heart was still heavy. I turned my eyes away from the Cross.

He led us around the rocky hill to a narrow path. There we found a garden that was hidden from the road. Scarlet anemones grew in the dewy grass beside the pathway. Yosef pointed down the path. "My new friend at the inn told me about this garden." We followed him as he talked. "He said over there is the cave where Joseph, the rich man, put Jesus' body. It was *his* new tomb."

I looked ahead to where the path ended. A low rectangular opening had been chiseled into the side of the hill. What looked like an absolutely unmovable round stone was leaning against the cave beside the entrance.

One at a time, we went inside the tomb. Waiting for my turn, I studied the huge stone. Something just as unmovable, solid, and weighty had settled down on my heart.

When it was my turn, I ducked in. I was alone inside His tomb. Yellowish Jerusalem dust motes floated in the shafts of light that played over the floor and hewed-out platform in front of me. *What a sad thing a tomb is.*

All alone in His tomb. The filtering bright sunlight coming from the doorway didn't overcome the feeling that it was a dark place. And it was deathly quiet.

Suddenly a thought flashed through my mind—a reminder of something I already knew. I was all alone in His tomb. No body lay on that slab. He was no longer dead. He got up and walked out of here!

My heart reached out for Him. *Jesus, it's all right, isn't it?* That's when I felt the absolutely unmovable stone roll right off my heart.

CHAPTER ELEVEN

THE PROMISE IS GIVEN

SIMON Peter's voice boomed out over the room. "Sit down, everyone, and let's get back to seeking the Lord."

As we found our seats, he began to pray. "Jesus we're waiting for Your promise. We miss You, Savior, and we've tarried in Jerusalem, just as You said, Lord. How we desire for You to send us our Comforter!"

Gathered with us in the open upstairs room were more than a hundred other believers. Jesus' disciples, His mother, and many others had been meeting here for over a week. They may have felt impatient and discouraged, but I was glad the Lord had given us time to get here.

We had gone back to the inn after our visit to Jesus' tomb. Eema expressed it for all of us when she said, "Please, may I rest in the quiet for a while? I can't stand the crowds now, Jonathan." Seeing Jesus' cross and tomb had changed our view of Jerusalem—if Jesus didn't fit in, then neither did we!

Later that afternoon Abba, Yosef, and David went to the temple to present their offerings to the Lord. They went into the Court of the Israelites, the closest any Jew but a priest could get to the Holy of Holies. The sanctuary was crowded with Jewish men. In a corner of the porch, they saw a group Abba recognized as Jesus' disciples. They were kneeling unashamedly and praying, while most of the other Jews were visiting with each other.

Abba motioned to Yosef and David, and they joined them. When their prayer ended, one of them spoke to Abba, "Brothers, will you come with us to the upper room? We are tarrying there for the Lord to send us His promise." How Abba must have rejoiced when he heard that! They followed the disciples to the upstairs room, and after explaining about us, they returned to the inn.

Looking out the window, I saw Abba hurrying down the street in our direction. He called, "We've found them. Get ready. We know where to go!"

I marveled how the Lord had guided their steps. *Oh, thank you, dear Jesus!*

We ate a hurried meal at the inn then set out through the crowded streets for the upper room. Abba led us to an old building made of Jerusalem stone whose second story had many open-air windows. We climbed the outside stairs and entered a hall two or three times larger than the dining room of Yosef's inn. Suddenly I saw Dod Micah. He was standing with a group of young men over by one of the windows.

When he saw us, his face lit up. He strode over to us, saying, "You've come! And as you can see, I've made it back!" He hugged Abba and Eema, and then took hold of me. Suddenly the room didn't seem strange anymore. I took one look at the excitement on Dod Micah's slender face and relaxed.

That's when Peter, seeming even taller than I remembered, called everyone back to prayer. David and I sat down between our eemas near the back of the room. Yosef, Abba, and Dod Micah found a welcome with the disciples and other men up near the front of the room.

It turned out that's where we spent the night.

How different it was to be in the midst of others who were as excited about Jesus as we were. I looked around and met the eyes of a girl about my age over by the window near our seats. She smiled and waved shyly. *I wonder how she met Jesus.* In the row behind us sat a cute little baby boy leaning on his eema's breast.

"Sister, my name is Ruth," whispered the older woman sitting beside Eema, "Where are you and your family from?" Eema told her and asked about her home. She began calling Eema, Sister Cilla, and me, Sister Lanee, and explained, "It's because Jesus has adopted us into His family." I, who have never had a brother or sister, was thrilled!

Sister Ruth knelt down in front of her chair and began praying a hole into Heaven. My, how she prayed! We sat listening then all of us knelt to pray. I tried to start praying, but it seemed hard among everyone. I turned my head and saw David's curly head resting on his folded arms. Then I heard him weeping as he prayed. I had never spent time this close to a boy. I surely had never heard one crying. It made me cry too. *Jesus, thank you for bringing David into my life. It feels like you've given me my very own brother.*

All through the long night, over a hundred others and I sent our prayers up to God's throne. Mostly I talked to Jesus about missing Him, and sometimes I told Him how great I felt just having the chance to be in this room waiting for Him to bless us. *Will you send us the promise tonight, Lord God?*

Too soon, I ran out of words and felt like I couldn't stay awake. It had grown quiet in the room. Prayers were whispers from every corner, with a fervent voice rising every now and then. Smoking lamps hanging against the plastered wall lit the room with soft cozy light.

David's elbow bumped my side and I awoke. He laughed when I sat up and said, "What?" He motioned to me, and we got up and walked to one of the nearby windows. Outside the city had lowered its lights for the night. I yawned, but felt refreshed from my nap.

"Lanee, what are we praying for?" David whispered in my ear.

"The *Promise*." I whispered back, looking at him as if he had fallen asleep with his eyes open.

"I know, but how will we know when we have it? What will it be like? Will we be able to see it, like we did Jesus?" David's expression grew more intense with every question.

I shook my head, for I didn't know any more than he did. His questions made me hungry to pray again. We knelt down by the window where the cool night air wafted into the room. I leaned my arms on the windowsill, looking out on the dim streets of Jerusalem. "Lord, send your people the help we need," I imagined all the girls lying on their mats out there that didn't know Jesus, and began to cry for their need. Then I thought of their eemas and abbas also sleeping their tiredness away below us and cried out for them to believe in the precious Savior. David, kneeling beside me, heard my prayer and began to pray the same way.

Our prayer was alive. We both stood up and lifted our hands to Jesus. The shy girl moved over by us. She lifted her hands and squeezed her eyes shut, calling out for His wonderful help. The whole room was coming alive again!

I heard voices up front and saw Peter and Andrew pacing across the front of the room, gesturing with their arms as they sought the Lord for His promise. Their rough fishermen's garb didn't match their words at all. "Lord Jesus, daystar in this dark world, Savior of all mankind, send us another Comforter," Peter prayed with His head thrust up toward the ceiling. Andrew, walking just behind his brother, cried out, "You always provided for us when we followed you. Provide for us now, dear Lord."

I kept on until I'd prayed all the desire of my heart out, then fell quiet. The baby boy awoke and cried, but soon his eema had him comforted. David and I went back over to our eemas and sat down. He leaned over and hummed a little tune in my ear, then sang,

> "When Jesus came, I was saved,
> When Jesus found me, I was freed,
> Since He came, I'm His child,
> He's supplying all my need."

I began to pick up the sweet melody and sing it with him quietly. Soon others around us joined in. We clapped an easy rhythm and sang the little song over and over. When we stopped, a beautiful strong bass voice began, "The Lord is my shepherd, I shall not want ..." We hundred and twenty believers sang of Jesus, the Good Shepherd, in the words of our king, the sweet Psalmist of Israel.

> He maketh me to lie down in green pastures:
> He leadeth me beside the still waters.
> He restoreth my soul:
> He leadeth me in the paths of righteousness
> for his name's sake.

Yea, though I walk through the valley of the
shadow of death,
I will fear no evil: for thou art with me;
Thy rod and thy staff they comfort me.
Thou preparest a table before me in the
presence of mine enemies:
Thou anointest my head with oil; my cup
runneth over.
Surely goodness and mercy shall follow me
all the days of my life:
And I will dwell in the house of the Lord forever.

With the last notes of the song, we began to praise the Good
Shepherd we knew face to face. I sat back down beside Eema
and heard her soft voice weeping before her Messiah. Recalling
Eema's smile when He said, "I am the good shepherd," I could
almost smell the sun-warmed grass of the field.

I tried to picture Jesus listening to us in Heaven. He would
be sitting on a golden throne. Certainly untold numbers of
angels in white robes were there worshiping Him. But, oh
my, it seemed that He wasn't listening to the angels, for His
ears were tuned to us in this room!

"Jesus, will you send us the promise now?" I whispered,
believing in Him more than I ever had. I remembered how
His hand felt on my head, when He blessed me with the
little ones. I thought of the little boy's comforted expression
when Jesus healed his stomach. Again, I heard the man cry,
"Look at me run! Look at me run!" Thoughts of His hands
scarred by nails, and of sharp thorns piercing His head
sifted through my mind. When I drifted into the silence of
the empty tomb, my eyelids drooped.

~~~

The sun's morning rays began spilling into the room. Many of us got up and moved around the now familiar room, trying to stretch the kinks out of our limbs. Dod Micah caught my eye across the room and sent me a smile and a wink. I sent the message back to him. When I looked at David, it seemed a squirrel had been nesting in his hair. As I smoothed it down for him, I wondered how mine looked.

Eema and I walked up to the front rows to give Abba a morning hug.

"I've never spent a night like that before!" he said as he hugged me. "How about you, Yonina?"

I smiled into his happy eyes, not really knowing how to answer him. I felt both tired and very excited.

Yosef sitting nearby with his tired eyes full of a dreamy expression said, "I will always remember our song in the night."

Just then, Peter, standing right beside us called out for everyone's attention. His tunic was wrinkled and his face looked weary. "May we pray one more time, dear brothers and sisters?"

We hurried back to our seats.

At first, the room grew quiet. I heard the birds singing their morning songs outside. The warm sunlight falling across my face reminded me that this was our holy day of the feast of Pentecost. The new thought seemed to banish my tiredness. *Oh my, the promise will come soon. I just know it! "Jesus, will you send us the promise, now?" I whispered, believing in Him more than I ever had.*

What started out as a low murmuring hum, began to be

everyone calling out to Jesus. The disciples and all the men up front stood and raised their hands as one, praying with loud and strong voices. Sitting near the back of the room, we saw the room sprout lifted arms until almost everyone was praying with their hands raised.

That's when I realized that something had happened to us in the night. We had lost our shyness of each other— we were no longer afraid to hear our own voice above the others'.

The baby's mother with him perched on her hip called, "Oh, Jesus, send us your promise!"

My brother David raised his voice and prayed, "Jesus, no one has ever helped me like you have. How I need your promise!"

From up front, I heard Jesus' disciple, Nathaniel, cry out, "Lord, you said you would never leave us comfortless, that you would come to us!"

Dod Micah said with tears, "Look down upon us, dear Savior. We want you and the Comforter!"

The individual voices shot up like sparks. Underneath everyone was pressing up toward that place where Jesus was, fervently seeking His answer.

Sister Ruth, sprawled on the floor with her arms wrapped around her chair bottom, cried out, "You have always kept your promises, Lord God!'

I heard Eema Lira praising the Lord with a little leap as if to get closer to Jesus, "Oh, my Lord, you have given me joy like I've never known!"

I heard Abba's deep musical voice, "Precious Messiah, fill our lives with your Comforter!"

Then I cried aloud, as one with the others, "Jesus, Lord Jesus, send us the promise!"

"AND SUDDENLY THERE CAME A SOUND FROM HEAVEN AS OF A RUSHING MIGHTY WIND, AND IT FILLED THE HOUSE WHERE THEY WERE SITTING!"

It screamed like a whirlwind barreling toward us, even though the windows still poured sunshine into the room. It drew closer and louder—an enormous whooshing sound powerful enough to blow down the house. It didn't stop for the ceiling; neither did it blow the ceiling down on us. No, it came right *through* it to us.

The wind filled up my ears, then was gone.

What's happening? That was my thought, but out of my mouth came strange words! Then I realized I wasn't the only one it was happening to—an indescribable noise filled the room. It was all our voices loudly speaking words I couldn't understand at all! Why was everyone uttering such strange sounds? Sister Ruth and Eema beside me, David and Eema Lira on the other side were babbling and looking astonished at themselves.

Up toward the disciples and Abba, I saw fire! Flickering orange flames were burning on their heads, and they didn't even seem to notice it! Surely, it wasn't burning them! The fire flamed up all around me. My eema's head and shoulders were bathed in the fire as she fervently spoke in an unknown tongue. Eema Lira's voice still held the joyful sound of praise, only in a strange language, as a large flame flared up from her shoulder. David lifted his worship to Jesus in a new tongue while glowing fire was all over his head. The words I spoke, though I didn't know what they meant, felt like they were coming right out of my heart. I looked through light as if a lamp was perched on my head and knew the fire was on me too!

The fire had caught everyone's attention! Wide-eyed with wonder, we began to grasp that the Lord had sent this amazing thing, and suddenly a dam of joy broke over us. Someone opened the door, and we began spilling down the stairs into the street, still speaking in strange languages.

When I got outside, another crowd was gathering around us. I felt so happy, it didn't matter who was nearby. I just let my mouth fly open to speak the new words. I didn't want it to stop! Somehow, every time I spoke there bubbled up in me love for Jesus and a feeling that God was right inside of me—it was the *Promise*!

As I continued to utter the strange new words, a trembling old man wrapped in a prayer shawl approached me and held his ear down near my face. With an awed look, he declared, "This girl is speaking in the language of my homeland! She is saying, 'God has sent His precious Son to save our souls!'"

"Can't you see they're all drunk?" an angry man's voice bellowed from the crowd.

That's when Peter stood up at the top of the stairs and began preaching. "These are not drunken as ye suppose, seeing it is but the third hour of the day. But this is that which was spoken by the prophet Joel, '… in the last days I will pour out my spirit upon all flesh.'"

Then I heard him preach that Jesus was "'exalted at the Father's right hand, and having received of the Father the promise of the Holy Ghost, he hath shed forth this, which ye now see and hear.'"

I thought, *Oh, Jesus, you did hear us up there in Heaven!* The news must have flashed over the city. The streets connected to our upper room were flooded with people.

Peter preached on, "Therefore let all the house of Israel know assuredly, that God hath made that same Jesus, whom ye crucified, both Lord and Christ."

I saw the people around me flinch as if they'd been struck. Perhaps some of them had cried not long ago, "Crucify Him! Crucify Him!"

"Men and brethren, what shall we do?" a man in the crowd raised his voice and asked fearfully.

"Repent and be baptized every one of you in the name of Jesus Christ for the remission of sins," Peter answered, "and ye shall receive the gift of the Holy Ghost." He went on preaching God's Word to them with his powerful voice, and soon hundreds were kneeling on the rough street crying out to the God of their fathers.

I watched David wading his way toward me through the river of people. His eyes met mine. They were full of the fire God had poured out. When he reached me, he took both my hands in his, saying, "Jesus has filled me with the Holy Ghost and fire, and has given me power to tell the world about His love. I never expected such a blessing. Oh, Lanee, whether Roman or Jew, now I'm truly one of His!" He let go of my hands and lifted his arms to the Lord, worshiping Him again in a strange language.

I felt my tears start. In the middle of the street in our great city of Jerusalem, I cried out with all of my heart, "Oh, thank you, Jesus, for sending us the Promise. Oh, yes, thank you for sending us Heaven's sweet Holy Ghost!"

CHAPTER TWELVE

SCRIBES FOR JESUS

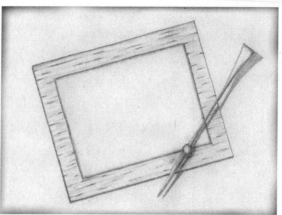

HOW do I express what has happened to me? The best way I can tell it is to say, I'm in a new world. When the rushing mighty wind blew through the upper room yesterday, it blew right through my soul. I've always believed that God is real. Now I am part of the God that is real. Oh, yes, a very human part, but truly part.

The hundred and twenty of us who experienced the outpouring of the Holy Ghost continued to worship there on the street while thousands of others turned to Jesus. After Peter preached, hundreds of men bent over the cobblestones crying out in abject repentance, "Lord, forgive me for all my sins, and fill *me* with the Holy Ghost!" God had made them hungry!

"Do you want Jesus to save you?" I asked a gray-haired man with tears rolling down his broad cheeks.

He nodded, and sobbed toward Heaven, "I knew it was wrong to crucify you, Jesus. Please forgive me for crying out for you to be killed. I knew it was wrong!"

I prayed for him with my hand resting on his stiff silver hair. The Holy Ghost began to speak through me. I felt a spark run down my arm into him. His arms flew up, and he began crying out for joy! *What forgiveness, Lord Jesus!*

I turned toward a pretty girl kneeling on the hard pavement. She wasn't crying. She held her head down and waited. I thought, *she wants me to touch her.* I remembered my prayer in the night and believed the Lord when my hand connected with her smooth black hair. All of a sudden, her arms shot up and the tears began flowing. She cried, "Oh, I can feel you, too. Oh! You love even me, Lord!"

All day long, we hundred and twenty prayed among them, for the power of the Holy Ghost was still mighty upon us! They felt Him, too. It was His great power, or, as I heard one of the disciples call it, His *anointing,* that brought such sorrow and yearning for God upon the people, and such power to save them when they cried out.

I had been praying for hours for scores of people when I happened near the edge of the seekers. I was surprised to see a familiar face watching from the crowd of spectators. He wasn't repenting. He wasn't praying for anyone. He was just watching. It was Rabbi ben Tzadik. How could I not know his red hair and freckled face? I thought he saw me recognize him, for he turned and plowed his way back out of the crowd. I stood for a moment watching him go, and then reached out to another young girl who was weeping before the Lord.

It was late afternoon before the great meeting was over. Abba and Eema joined me, and we climbed back up the stone stairs looking for Yosef and the others. We found them in the upper room listening to Jesus' disciple, John. He was a young man in his twenties with a wiry sunlit beard and unruly hair to match. His sincere voice was much quieter than Peter's.

"Thousands have come to Jesus today. Tomorrow some of us disciples will begin baptizing the new believers. The rest will stay here and tell you about our time with Jesus." John said, with eyes still full of Holy Ghost fire. "Pass the word for all of the hundred and twenty who can write to bring writing materials here. Let's begin at the third hour."

Dod Micah walked with us back to our inn. "I knew God wanted you to come, Lanee!" he said with his arm draped around my shoulders. "You'll be a great witness for Jesus back in Arbela now that you're filled with the Holy Ghost."

"What are your plans, Dod?"

"I know the Lord wants me to stay here for now with the disciples. We are going to face a time of persecution soon. The High Priest and Temple rulers won't take this great move of God without trying to put a stop to it." He saw my worried expression and added, "Never fear, my little niece, Jesus will help us through it all."

He ate supper with us then left for his house in Bethany, promising to meet us the next morning. We went to our couches before the sun went down—happy, excited, and oh, so tired.

Early the next morning we left for the market to buy some wax tablets and styluses. The marketplace was just coming alive with the bleating of many sheep, the clucking of chickens, and the cheerful calls of vendors greeting one another. Someone was pleasantly accompanying all this with a pretty song on a flute.

Our first stop was at a wagonload of green striped melons, red and yellow mangoes, waxy orange persimmons, and sunny lemons tended by a stocky farmer with a balding head fringed with gray hair. Yosef thumped a melon, paid for it, and requested the vendor slice it for him.

We strolled on to the source of the delicious aroma of fresh bread. The baker, a sturdy woman with a floured apron, stood beaming over her tables of buns and fragrant sweet cakes. "Come, buy the freshest bread in the market!" she coaxed. Her hair was done up in as neat a bun as the ones on the table. Abba pointed to some soft white rolls. She handed each of us one, then accepted Abba's money with a glowing smile.

We found a table near the milk vendor. Abba purchased milk and cheese to complete our breakfast. We all bowed our heads and gave thanks then dug in to the feast. How creamy was the cheese, the roll was just as good as I remembered, and the fresh crisp melon was oh, so refreshing.

When we finished we walked deeper into the amazing spectacle of color and stuff—Jerusalem's market.

"Look, Eema!" I cried, when I saw the lovely ready-made tunics and scarves on display outside of a booth. They were just like the one Deborah wore to the feast—and very expensive.

When Eema came to a yarn shop, she went in and picked out a skein of a most striking shade of blue yarn. I'd seen the lake water shine that color on bright summer days. When

Abba bought it for her, she tucked it into her bag without saying what she planned to make it into.

Up ahead we saw what we'd been looking for—a kiosk overflowing with household items. "Come in! Come in! We have everything you could ever want or need!" the owner called out and we all squeezed in. There beside the brass pots was a large stack of wax tablets and a variety of metal styluses. We bought the whole stack of tablets and a stylus apiece.

I remembered Savta's patient instruction as I picked out a pretty copper stylus. David and Eema Lira laughed together recalling their many nights alone practicing their writing. What words we'd soon be writing!

With all we needed in hand, we turned away from the bustling marketplace and headed back to our upper room. The familiar stone stairs led us back into the sacred aura of Jesus' people.

We found the disciples had divided up to tell their stories. Abba sent David and me to hear John. He was standing over by the window where David and I had prayed so earnestly for the promise. *Now we have it!* As we waited with the many others for him to begin, I noticed Dod Micah coming in the door loaded down with tablets. He nodded and smiled, then joined Matthew's group near the door.

John began to speak in his low voice. I moved up closer, as did David and the others. A friendly smile lit John's boyish features. I realized I was smiling too—and no wonder after what had happened yesterday—*you sent us the promise, Lord!*

John started the story. "It was John the Baptist who introduced me to Jesus—for I had met John first. I came to John the Baptist hoping that *he* was the Messiah; but he said, no, someone mightier than he should come. Andrew, over there, and I were at John's meeting at the Jordan that day, when he pointed out Jesus and said, 'Behold the Lamb of God!'

"Thinking Jesus must be the Messiah, we left John at the Jordan and followed after Him. We didn't really want Jesus to see us following, so we trailed way behind Him, making every turn He did. Suddenly He stopped, turned, and faced us. As we came closer He asked, 'Whom seek ye?' By His tone I knew He wasn't angry at us, so I up and said, 'Rabbi, where do you live?'" John smiled as he remembered it, his rosy lips parting over some crooked teeth. "He, as friendly as could be, said, 'Come and see.'

"After that He gathered up us disciples until there were twelve. We four, Peter and Andrew, James and I, left our fishing boats the day He came by and said, 'Follow me, and I will make you fishers of men.' From then on, I followed Him wherever He would let me go."

John watched us finish writing that down, and then continued. "Though I wasn't there the night He met the rich and powerful Nicodemus, Jesus told me all about it, and I believe He wants me to tell it to you, so you can share it with others.

"Begin writing this down: Jesus was on the rooftop of His friend's house late one night, when Nicodemus, a ruler of the Jews came. He asked Jesus, 'Rabbi, we know that thou art a teacher come from God: for no man can do the miracles that thou doest except God be with him.'

"Jesus answered him, 'Verily, verily, I say unto thee, except a man be born again, he cannot see the Kingdom of God '"

As I wrote this down, I thought, *I have never heard about being born again! What did Jesus mean?*

John's soft voice continued, "Nicodemus asked him, 'How can a man be born when he is old? Can he enter the second time into his mother's womb and be born?'"

I'm so glad you asked, Nicodemus.

"Jesus answered him, 'Verily, verily, I say unto thee, Except a man be born of water and of the Spirit, he cannot enter into the Kingdom of God, That which is born of the flesh is flesh; and that which is born of the Spirit is spirit.'"

John stopped right there and asked, "Did you get all that?" The gray-haired man next to me asked him to repeat a part. I had never written so fast. The point of my copper stylus scratched away the flat wax, leaving the words perfectly legible. I tried to write small so I could get more on the tablet.

When John was satisfied that we'd written all that down, he resumed his recital. "'Marvel not that I said unto thee, Ye must be born again,' Jesus said to Nicodemus, 'The wind bloweth where it listeth, and thou hearest the sound thereof, but canst not tell whence it cometh, and whither it goeth: so is every one that is born of the Spirit.'"

David and I finished writing and raised our heads. The young disciple's expression had deepened, as if Jesus' words were affecting him. I didn't try to write then; I watched John. He stood thinking and reacting to His thoughts—it seemed his face was bathed in internal sunlight.

I looked back down at the words I'd just written, "the wind bloweth where it listeth ... so is every one that is born of the Spirit." *Oh, He is speaking of the wind that blew through this room yesterday morning!* With that thought, the Holy Ghost came upon me, and I began to speak in the unknown tongue I was given yesterday. Again! I rejoiced that the promise was still with me. The next moment He came upon John, too! Then David and the rest of the group were moved on by the Spirit.

The wind blew over the whole room. There was no outside wind or fire, for, I realized, it had move *into* our hearts: we yielded and the power of the Holy Ghost once more caused us to speak in strange languages as the Spirit gave the words. He filled me with joy, even as He did yesterday.

At first, John spoke in those strange languages with us, and then suddenly he raised his voice and began to speak words we could understand. Everyone in all the groups quieted to hear as he continued his narrative.

"Nicodemus asked Jesus, 'How can these things be?'"

I noticed David was writing again, so I picked up my stylus, too. "Jesus answered him, 'Art thou a master of Israel and knowest not these things? Verily, verily, I say unto thee, we speak that we do know, and testify that we have seen; and ye receive not our witness. If I have told you earthly things and ye believe not, how shall ye believe, if I tell you of heavenly things?

"'And no man hath ascended up to Heaven, but he that came down from Heaven. And as Moses lifted up the serpent in the wilderness, even so must the Son of man be lifted up: that whosoever believeth in him should not perish, but have eternal life.'"

John paused, the fire burning in his eyes. Surely, the Holy Ghost was pouring the words into his heart. He paused for a few moments allowing us to catch up. Then John's voice sounded to every corner of the room, "'For God so loved the world, that he gave his only begotten Son, that whosoever believeth in him should not perish, but have everlasting life.'"

A room full of styluses marked John's inspired words onto the wax tablets.

Quieter, John then said, "'For God sent not his Son into the world to condemn the world; but that the world through him might be saved. He that believeth on him is not condemned: but he that believeth not is condemned already, because he hath not believed in the name of the only begotten Son of God.'"

He waited. Our styluses worked across the wax tablets—I grabbed another one.

He spoke again, "'And this is condemnation, that light is come into the world, and men loved darkness rather than light, because their deeds were evil. For every one that doeth evil hateth the light neither cometh to the light, lest his deeds be reproved.'"

I got it down, glanced up, and saw the light of inspiration still in his eyes. He continued, "'But he that doeth truth cometh to the light, that his deeds may be made manifest, that they are wrought in God.'"

Then he stopped. We finished.

We sat soaking in the words that Jesus had spoken. We all had them. We could carry them home with us and tell them to everyone around us. Would they believe?

CHAPTER THIRTEEN
SAVTA IS DYING!

WHAT marvelous acts and astounding wisdom we heard all that day in the upper room! The disciples dictated for hours sermons that Jesus had preached and great miracles He had performed. We got back to the inn with our arms loaded down with treasures—the wax tablets full of words.

In the courtyard of the inn, we were surprised to see Dod Ethan! Abba handed David his tablets and ran to his brother-in-law, who was pacing up and down the courtyard.

"Ethan, why are you here? Has something happened?"

Dod Ethan stopped pacing and cried, "Thanks be to God, you've come, Jonathan—your eema is gravely ill! We must return to Arbela tonight. I've traveled day and night to try to reach you before she leaves us!" Suddenly his tired face wrinkled up and he began to weep.

Abba's face turned pale at the news. When he put his arms around Dod Ethan, he squeezed his eyes shut and tears rolled down his cheeks.

Oh, no. Savta doesn't believe in Jesus. She mustn't die now—she'll be lost! Then I started to cry.

When Abba let go of Dod Ethan, Dod pulled a handkerchief from his girdle and blew his nose, and said, "I went to Micah's bakery and he wasn't there. His hired man told me you were staying at this inn. I'm so glad I found you. Can we leave at once?"

Abba dried his face on his sleeve and asked Yosef in a shaken voice, "How long before you can be ready to go?"

"I'm going to the stable now to get the donkeys and wagon prepared." He took David to help. Our eemas and I left to gather our things from the rooms.

Soon we were packed and ready to leave. Yosef had arranged for Eema Lira and David to stay a few more days at the inn until they finished the dictations. "By then," David said, "the Lord will help us know which direction to take."

It was hard for me to leave them behind—we had all grown so close in the last week.

Dod Ethan had ridden to Jerusalem on Yosef's beautiful sorrel stallion. "It was the fastest way I could think of to get here. When I explained the need to your watchman, he saddled him up and sent me along. But Yosef, he's give out. I'll hire a horse for Jonathan to ride ahead. I'll also hire a donkey for me and you can ride your horse home slowly, with Lanee and Cilla driving the wagon."

I knew Abba was very worried about Savta when he agreed. He kissed us, waved goodbye to the rest, and began the long ride to Arbela. Yosef had slung a pouch of food and a skin of water over the horse's rump. He loaded food and water in our wagon, too. His friend the innkeeper had proved himself a great help with these last minute needs.

"Goodbye David. I hope we will meet again." My eyes flooded once again with tears. I didn't want to leave my new friend behind. Standing in the lamplight, I studied his dear face, wanting to remember every detail.

He must have felt the same way, for he touched my hair and gave me a sympathetic smile. "Goodbye *for now,* Lanee.

We will be praying for your savta. Don't forget to trust in Jesus as you go." He helped me up into the wagon and squeezed my hand before he let it go.

Eema kissed Eema Lira then David helped her up into the wagon. Eema Lira smiled up at me, and I leaned down for her kiss. As we started out on the long road home, I turned back and saw them in the lamplight waving good bye. *Jesus, will I ever see David again?*

Eema drove the wagon out of Jerusalem's gates following Dod Ethan and Yosef on their mounts. With all of us riding, the trip should be much faster than when we'd come.

I called out, "Yosef, please forgive me for asking, but didn't you say that traveling at night is dangerous because of robbers?" I didn't want to be afraid, but he *had* said it.

He turned around in his saddle and answered, "We must travel at night, daughter, and we must depend on our Lord to see us safely home to your savta."

Yosef's faith eased my fears.

I found out I liked traveling at night. It was so cool. I crawled back into the wagon bed and pulled a blanket out of my clothes bag. I dragged it back to the seat beside Eema and we wrapped it around our shoulders. The wagon rattled over the dark stony road with only the moon to light our path. Eema and I began praying for Abba riding ahead of us and for Savta not to die. I remembered when she was well and taught us young girls of our village. We met at her house every morning but the Sabbath. She was a patient, interesting teacher. I was always proud that our teacher was *my* grandmother. I knew she was sick, but I had never thought she would die!

Lord Jesus, please don't let my savta die! I felt like my heart would break every time I thought about her dying without believing in Jesus. *Have mercy, dear Lord!*

We stopped after several hours and fed the horse and donkeys. We were so glad for the supper our good innkeeper had packed us—a whole roasted chicken, bread smeared with rich butter and honey, and a large cluster of grapes.

"Ethan, why do you think Savta is so critically ill?" Eema asked. "When we left home, she seemed to be feeling some better." We were sitting on a blanket near the back wagon wheel, leaning against it as we ate. Yosef hadn't wanted to build a fire and maybe attract any highway robbers' attention. He stood guard at the back of the wagon.

Dod Ethan was lying down in the wagon bed. He had only eaten a little. Having no sleep for many nights, he wearily answered her, "I don't know, Cilla. When I finally decided to come for Jonathan, she was gasping for every breath. Her lips were blue and she was too weak to sit up. Ruth was afraid, for she'd never seen her that sick. I hated to leave them, but I couldn't let anything happen without Jonathan being there." He paused then said in a sad voice, "It's possible for him to ride it in two days—that's how long it took me. I just hope he's not too late."

For a few minutes, we sat listening to the crickets. Then we heard Dod Ethan's snoring begin above us in the wagon.

Yosef, from the back of the wagon, said quietly, "Let's ask Jesus to help your savta."

We three knelt by the wagon, crying out softly for our Savior to go to Savta and help her. Suddenly the Holy Ghost began to speak through us. He took hold of my tongue and prayed the words for Savta that I didn't know how to pray. I knew He was asking the Lord God in just the right words for her help. How did I know that? I'm not sure, but somehow I understood it. And not just I, but also Eema and Yosef did. We began praising the Lord as quietly as we could, when all three of us realized that Savta would not die!

I guess we weren't very quiet, for suddenly Dod Ethan sat up in the wagon.

"What was that?" he asked, now fully awake.

At first, we just looked at each other and said nothing. An owl hooted off somewhere in the night. Then Yosef stood up and said, "You mean, when we said words you didn't understand?"

"Yes! What was that? I thought I was dreaming, but I wasn't, was I? You were all speaking words that I couldn't understand."

Eema and I stood up, and I said, "It's the Holy Ghost, Dod Ethan."

"Do you mean God's Spirit? Is He causing you to speak words like that?" His eyes were wide, and he seemed a little afraid.

Yosef leaned his strong old arms on the tailgate and said, "Ethan, what we have, we got from Jesus. Do you want to know Jesus Christ as your Savior?"

Dod looked into Yosef's watery eyes, and I held my breath. He seemed almost timid when he quietly said, "Yes."

"Jesus preached, 'Repent and believe the gospel—believe the good news that Jesus gave His life to wash you clean in His blood from all sin." Yosef's eyes were locked into Dod's.

Finally, Dod Ethan dropped his eyes to the floor boards of the wagon. He sounded nervous when he spoke again.

"I-I'm sorry I crucified you, Jesus ..." A heavy sigh came from him then he began again. "I-I'm sorry I have spent my whole life only seeking riches for myself. And for craving the approval of others. I know Yosef, Cilla, and Lanee have something I have never known. If only *I* could have what they have! Oh ... Lord ... yes, *Lord* Jesus, please forgive me, and please wash me in your blood—the blood you shed when I crucified you!"

Dod lifted his eyes to Heaven. With tears running down his cheeks, he suddenly uttered a cry of sorrow that seemed to erupt from the bottom of his soul, "Argh!" We waited as he quieted down, and then we saw him lie back in the wagon and close his eyes.

Still we waited until we heard his soft snoring begin. The crickets sang to us there in the quiet night. It was the sweetest night sound I'd ever heard. For tonight, Dod Ethan had found peace.

CHAPTER FOURTEEN

SAVTA MEETS JESUS

J UST as the Holy Ghost had assured us, Savta was much
    better when we reached Arbela. As we turned off the
    main road toward home, we saw a horse galloping our
way. The rider waved as he came. Finally, we could see the
big smile on the rider's face—it was Abba!

"The Lord touched Savta. She is alive!" he yelled as he
neared us. We all waved and nodded.

"We know, Abba," I told him as he rode up beside the
wagon. "The disciples told us the Holy Ghost would show
us things to come, and He surely did. We knew Savta was
better. When we prayed, He showed us."

I stopped the donkeys, and Eema and I jumped down to hug
Abba. Pressed up against his rough tunic, I smelled Eema's
soap mixed up with the smell of work—my Abba's smell!

He squeezed me close, then said over my head, "Ethan,
want to get there a little faster? She's a fine mount you hired
me!" Abba let go of me and held out the black mare's reins.
Dod dismounted the donkey, and with an ear-to-ear grin
grabbed Abba and hugged him, too.

Surprised, Abba said, "What's happened?"

We all laughed.

"Sounds like all of you had an enjoyable trip."

Dod Ethan said, "I'm born again."

I've seen Abba grin before, but never like he did when he
heard that! We all started laughing again then we lifted our

hands and praised our dear Lord. Dod Ethan's glad voice was loudest of us all. After that, he rode off toward Savta's to share his good news with Dodah Ruth.

We proceeded slowly until Yosef turned off toward the inn. "We'll bring you the wagon tomorrow, Yosef," Abba said. Then, guess what? I got to ride Dod's donkey so Eema and Abba could ride together in the wagon. They talked with their heads together, while I bounced along on the back of a *race donkey!* He wanted to go faster and faster. I tried to stay beside the wagon, but he didn't want to go that slow.

"Abba, may I ride on ahead?" I asked, wanting to feel just how fast he could run.

"Can you handle him, Lanee?"

"I believe so."

"All right, but don't let that little scoundrel throw you."

I nudged him in the sides, and we took off! I wanted to cry, "Help, Abba!" but there wasn't time. I could tell the donkey was enjoying the run, as I managed somehow to keep my seat. Finally, I saw Savta's stone fence coming toward us and pulled on the reins. He instantly obeyed and almost threw me over his head. I got off.

Abba and Eema came on down the road in the wagon. I saw a concerned look on her face, while Abba tried to hide his grin behind his hand. I walked with them into Savta's with wobbly legs.

Savta was reclining on the red and gold cushions of her couch when we entered. Her eyes, at first weak and tired, grew bright when she saw us. She held her hands out to us.

"Lanee and Cilla, how I missed you two." Her voice wasn't

strong. I kissed her soft cheek. *Thank you, Lord for helping her live!*

Dodah Ruth came in, kissing as she went. The Jews, it is said, are a very affectionate people. Dodah Ruth always confirms it, if there is ever a doubt. She loved us sufficiently, petting my hair and kissing Eema twice. Then she said, "Now we'll let Savta rest. She is still not strong—better every day—but still not strong."

We ate a delicious supper of Dodah Ruth's mutton stew and caraway bread then Abba took us home. Abba tied the donkey behind the wagon, for I needed to lead Nanny Goat and her kids home. I remembered the trouble I had getting them to Savta's before we left. Nanny wanted to graze, the kids wanted to explore. This time I was prepared. "Come on Nanny, come on rascals. Get your treat!" The carrots Dodah Ruth gave me worked just great all the way home.

Home! The old sycamore tree's mottled trunk stood guard in front with its fallen leaves crowded around the front door. I led the goats through the side gate and left them. Inside the back door, I took a moment to delight in the smell of our own house. It was a spicy, earthy, lovely smell. I hastily washed up in the kettle of rainwater by the back door. Brushing Eema and Abba's face with a kiss, I carried my lamp up the stairs to my room. The dancing shadows on the plaster walls welcomed me. I undressed and slipped on my old tunic that hung on its peg. With a happy sigh, I blew out the light and stretched out on *my* mat. My comfortable mat, in my room, in my home. Never had I experienced such a trip, but oh, how good it was to be home.

Savta improved daily. The next week Dod Ethan and his

family returned to Jerusalem. Before he left, he promised to see David and Eema Lira if they were still there, and tell them how Savta was recovering. He also said he would seek out the Lord's followers and join them, but asked us to pray for him. He knew a believer in Jesus would probably not last long on the Sanhedrin. When he said this, he didn't look sorry. He still had peace.

Life seemed to return to normal then. Yosef re-opened the inn, and Abba went back to work every day. Eema and I took turns spending the nights and days with Savta. At night, we gathered at her house for supper. She didn't object when Abba blessed the food in the name of Jesus. Actually, she didn't talk much at all. Whole days I cared for her and her house, and she hardly spoke a word. I asked Eema about it. She said, "Maybe her sickness took a lot out of her."

It was several weeks after Pentecost, and my turn to spend the night with Savta. I had a mat on the other side of her room, near the door to the courtyard. We had settled in for the night. I lay awake thinking Savta had fallen asleep. Her side of the room was very quiet. I turned over to look out on the courtyard from my mat. The night was dark. I heard Savta's cow moving around out there.

Jesus? I love you. Will you watch over Eema and Abba tonight? And remember Yosef, David, and Eema Lira. And Jesus, please show Ben who you are.

"Lanee."

Her voice made me jump. When I recovered, I said, "Yes, Savta."

"What happened to my family in Jerusalem?"

"Uh ... Savta, did you ask Abba?"

"No, granddaughter, I'm asking *you*. What happened that makes me feel outside of you all? Even Ethan. He seemed happier that I've ever seen him before he left this time, but he seemed to be in a different world than I am. I want to know what happened to you all."

"Are you sure you want to talk about it, Savta—it is about Jesus."

"I know that much, child, I'm not blind. Tell me what happened."

So lying on my mat, I told her everything—about Yosef finding Jesus, about meeting David and Eema Lira, and David's story. Then I told her about seeing the Cross on the hill and the empty tomb. Finally, in the dark room I relived the night we spent in the upper room, describing how it felt to pray throughout the night for the Lord's promise.

She didn't say a word through all that I said.

I continued, "Suddenly, I began to speak in a language I did not know, Savta. I saw fire on the heads and shoulders of everyone, but it wasn't burning them. They, too were speaking in unknown tongues—Eema, Abba, Yosef, David, Eema Lira, and Dod Micah, too! It was wonderful! We ended up on the streets of Jerusalem, and thousands of people who had come to the feast of Pentecost gathered around us. Peter, Jesus' disciple, preached, and I've heard that three thousand of them came to believe in Jesus that day. Savta, the promise Jesus sent is the outpouring of the Holy Ghost!"

Then I stopped talking, not sure what to say next. Minutes passed.

"Lanee?"

"Yes, Savta."

"I almost died a few days ago," she said with a slight tremble in her words. "It was dark inside me, and I was sinking into the blackness. Then I heard a voice. It was unlike any voice I'd ever heard, but it seemed familiar to me. The voice said, 'Don't reject me,' I wondered who it was. Suddenly I remembered your face when I was angry that you were going to see Jesus. Then I knew.

"Oh, Savta, will you be like us? Will you be His, too?"

I heard her turning toward me on her couch. She said, "Please come over here near me, Lanee." I quickly went to her bed and got down on my knees beside her.

She reached for my hand. Her hand felt warm and strong. "Will you forgive me?" I couldn't see her face, but I could hear sorrow in her voice. "I have been so set in my old age ways, that I almost missed my Lord's Son, and tried to prevent you from believing in Him. God has always meant everything to me. Or, that's what I thought. Now, I want it to really be true, as it is for my children."

I held Savta's hand to my cheek. Then I heard her say in her firm "Savta" voice, "Jesus, if you are listening to me, I want you to know I will never reject you again. I will be your loyal servant for the rest of my life and forever more. Please forgive me, my Lord."

When she finished, the Holy Ghost fell on us. On my savta and me. We both gave Him our tongues to glorify God in words we did not understand, that we could not have said without God's inspiration. I heard Savta's strong voice, and knew she was healed, and knew she was saved!

CHAPTER FIFTEEN
THE RABBI'S VISIT

FROM that night, Savta was well. The next morning she was up before I was, milking the cow. I awakened to voices praising God out in the courtyard. Abba must have stopped by on his way to work. The Holy Ghost was rejoicing through both of them quite loudly. I heard Abba's feet running around the courtyard and I knew his face was one ear-to-ear grin. Even the cow started bellowing. I jumped up, lifting my hands to Jesus, too.

We had to tell Eema! I pulled my tunic over my head and slipped into my sandals, taking a moment to smooth my hair before I joined them. The three of us hurried down the road then ran through the house into the back court. Eema was standing at the oven with her mouth wide open. I got the first word in. "Eema, look at Savta!"

"I'm healed, Cilla! I'm saved! I'm filled with the Holy Ghost!"

A cloudburst of joy followed. Eema and Savta hugged and laughed, while Abba and I worshiped the One who had done it.

Oh, what a sweet morning it is, Jesus!

At the inn, the same thing happened when we told Yosef. His special "I've heard from Jesus" smile beamed out while we shouted some more.

Lord Jesus, you've given me my savta back, and she's even better than before!

The Sabbath morning after she was saved, Savta walked

into the synagogue with us. It had been many Sabbaths since she had been able to go. Most everyone believed Savta would never recover from her sickness. Some of her old friends gathered around excited to see her up again.

I saw Rabbi ben Tzadik enter the side door of the synagogue preoccupied with straightening the sleeve of his embroidered robe. When he had it straight, he looked up and caught sight of Savta. He stopped in his tracks.

Since we'd believed in Jesus, the rabbi only spoke to us when we spoke to him. But Savta didn't know this. She had known our rabbi when he was a little boy, for he wasn't much older that Abba and Dodah Ruth. Savta had taken care of him sometimes so his parents could go to Jerusalem. When she lifted her eyes and saw him standing there, she excused herself from the group and approached him saying, "How nice to see you this morning, Thaddaeus," in her very audible Savta voice.

You should have seen his face! His mouth fell open and his eyes bulged.

"Why Eema Rose, are you sure you are able to be here? Someone get her a chair!"

With a radiant smile she declared, "I feel very able, Thaddaeus, for Jesus Christ has healed me."

Suddenly the rabbi looked as if *he* needed a chair. He popped out in a sweat. Every conversation stopped.

Savta innocently continued, "And, I want to announce that I will re-open the school for our girls the Monday of next week. I will be teaching it for free to all girls above six years old. We will begin at the third hour and end at the seventh each day but the Sabbath, of course."

We expected him to react to Savta's remarks, but it didn't happen. Our rabbi turned and walked to the pulpit, so everyone hurried to their seats.

He led the service with his same form and dignity, only he had a certain tightness around his mouth and eyes I hadn't seen before. Maybe it would have been better if he'd said something.

As his voice rose and fell reading the Scriptures, I recalled seeing him on the streets of Jerusalem. Our rabbi wasn't acknowledging Savta's healing today, just as he'd never mentioned seeing me full of the Holy Ghost helping others seek the Lord *that day.* When I told Abba and Eema I'd seen him watching us, Abba said we'd just wait to see what happened. *It seems our rabbi is just ignoring us, Lord.*

When the service ended, he went straight to the side door and disappeared. Sarah and her eema went to their regular spots at the front door, but our rabbi didn't show up.

"Hello, Sarah," I said, as I passed. "Will you be coming to school?"

She glanced at me then looked in the direction her abba had left and said, "I don't know."

When she looked back at me, I said, "I hope you will."

After all the excitement about Savta, I thought to look for Ben and his family in the crowd. I hadn't seen him since the feast. *They're not here again,* I thought, disappointed. *We've never had that after-the-service talk he'd asked me for.* I missed him.

The next day, Sunday, was becoming special in our home. We'd heard the disciples call it *the Lord's day,* because Jesus rose from the dead on the first day of the week. Abba said many believers had begun to hold that day apart to worship Him. Since we weren't allowed to mention Jesus in our synagogue, we decided to worship him together on Sunday, too. We read from the scrolls the things we'd copied from our tablets, sang some of the Psalms that prophesied of Jesus, and ended with prayer together. Yosef always came.

This first day of the week Savta came. Eema and I had cooked a special meal of roast chicken with buttery noodles to eat after the service. Abba started the service with a suggestion. "Cilla! Why don't we sing that new song you composed about how Jesus loves the little children?"

Eema went to get her tablet, and we all stood up waiting for her to teach it to us. In the lull, we heard footsteps coming up the road to our house. They were firm business-like steps. I peered out through the open doorway. *Oh no!* I must have looked shocked, for Abba turned and looked where I was looking. As he did, Rabbi ben Tzadik came to the sycamore tree then walked right up and stood in the doorway.

What a sight he was—red hair flaming over his hot red face. The richly embroidered robe covering him from wide shoulders to well-shod toe spoke authority in our humble living room. He glared around at each of us, then at our scrolls, and finally with a hard set to his jaw, he looked fully into Abba's face.

"Jonathan, may I have a word with you?"

Abba stared into his eyes for a moment, and then turned to Eema. "Go ahead without me, Cilla."

When they went outside, we tried to sing Eema's song. We

didn't do a very good job. "Jesus loves the tiny and small," Eema coached us. Savta, Yosef, and I had one ear on the song and one out the door. "Jesus loves the *sminy* and tall," I heard Yosef sing. It would have been funny any other time.

"Yes, Jesus loves the children everywhere!" we managed to finish together as Abba returned looking sad.

He saw our curious faces and said, "Let's all sit down."

"What is it, son?" Savta asked.

Abba sat down across from the four of us and gave us the bad news. "Eema, our rabbi has asked that we do not come to the synagogue anymore. He strongly opposes our belief in what he calls 'that deceiver,' and will not allow anyone to preach faith in Him in any form in the synagogue. He also said the parents will be forbidden to send their girls to your school."

"What did you tell him, Jonathan?" Yosef wanted to know.

"I said, 'They that believed as you do crucified Him. But, He rose again, Rabbi. We will do as you wish, but, Thaddaeus, you will not be able to stop this, for it is of God.'"

"Did that make him mad, Abba?"

"Perhaps, but all he said was, 'I do not agree, and will not allow you to spread this heresy in the synagogue. Goodbye, Jonathan.'"

We sat there stunned.

Then Savta said with a sigh, "I remember how cruel my unbelief was. But now—now, I see what I was once too blind to see." She gave Abba a small smile and said, "Jesus suffered for us, son. Didn't He?"

"Yes—much more than just being banned from the synagogue."

Trying to absorb the shock of our rabbi's rejection, none of us had any more words. Then suddenly, Yosef spoke up. "I have a superb idea!"

"What is it, Yosef?" Eema and I both asked at once. What could have turned Yosef's sad expression upside-down?

"I remember the disciples said that Jesus called the gathering of His believers, *His church*. He said, 'Upon this rock I will build my church and the gates of hell shall not prevail against it.' Why can't we be the church in Arbela, and why can't we meet on Sunday at the inn? I will close it for everything but church in the morning until noon."

Then he added, "And, Rose, though I doubt you will have any other students but Lanee, I offer you one of the inn's rooms for a schoolroom."

Abba and Eema's eyes looked interested, and Savta's smile really lit up. We all quickly agreed Yosef's plan was a wonderful idea.

Rabbi ben Tzadik would have been amazed if he could have seen us then. Instead of grieving over being branded a family of heretics, unhappily locked out of fellowship with the rest of the village, we were busy catching a vision of a new church with an open door for the Holy Ghost to guide us into worshiping our Lord!

The next day Yosef put a sign out in front of the Window Inn:

THE LORD'S DAY WORSHIP--HERE
SUNDAY--3RD HOUR TO 6TH HOUR
EVERYONE WELCOME
DINING ROOM RE-OPENS 7TH HOUR

Beside it, he posted another smaller sign:

ALL GIRLS FREE SCHOOL
ROOM BETH

Of course, I was the only girl who came that first day. It seemed strange to be the lone student. But Savta jumped right in, seeming to enjoy my being her entire class. After we prayed for the Lord's guidance, she began a history lesson by telling me a story.

"In my eema and abba's childhood a queen ruled our land. Her name was Alexandria. She became queen when her husband Alexander died. She was sixty-four years old and came into her power in a time of political unrest. Yet, Alexandria was able to do something of major importance for the Jewish people: she proclaimed that all the children of the land should be educated regardless of their sex."

Savta's earnest gray eyes held mine. "Lanee, she mandated that both the girls and the boys should learn to read and write, and to be taught history, mathematics, and geography. I am some of the fruit of her wise rule. I was allowed to learn academics, as well as to learn how to do things the girls have always done—milk the goats, spin the flax, cook a good stew."

She paused, and I asked, "Could your eema read and write, Savta?"

Savta's eyes grew wistful as she said, "No, though she was under Alexandria's rule, her mother thought it nonsense for girls to go to school. When I was born, my eema, though never allowed to herself, was anxious for me to study and learn. She sent me to school in the synagogue every day, handling the housework by herself most of the time. I was taught by our rabbi, who was Yosef's father.

"After I married your sabba, and had Jonathan and Ruth, I became the teacher of the girls in our village. I taught your eema and her sisters. Though you are my only student now, I believe I will teach others again—all because the Lord has healed me and saved me, and because of Yosef's 'superb idea.'"

We smiled at each other, remembering how Yosef's vision had picked us up. "I am grateful for good Queen Alexandria's short reign—it was only nine years. Because of her wisdom, I am not illiterate, and neither are you."

When the history lesson ended, Savta took me on a whirlwind review of what she had taught me before. That first week we began borrowing scrolls from Yosef for reading lessons and for Scripture studies. Savta told stories of her family who had died before I was born, especially of my grandfather who died when abba was a young boy. My sabba was a wonder with animals—he trained his housecats to come when he whistled and tamed a wild badger for a pet. School had become an adventure for me—with my new savta!

I went to the well after our third interesting school day. I hadn't run into any of the other girls since our visit from the rabbi. Maybe it was because I had purposely gone early for our water each day. I wasn't afraid of them—just nervous, and I wasn't ready for any of Sarah's haughty remarks.

This time when I arrived, I was surprised to see Deborah sitting under the date palm tree that shaded the well. I couldn't help myself—I laughed. When I did, that nervous feeling left.

She stood up and brushed off her silk skirt. "What are you laughing about, Lanee?"

"I apologize—it just struck me funny that you, Deborah, were sitting under a palm tree, just like the Deborah of the Scriptures did. Remember how she was one of the judges of our nation? Are you going to judge me, Deborah?" Then I gave her a friendly, "just teasing" smile.

"Sometimes, I just can't figure you out," she said. "I thought you'd be distressed, or at least a little troubled that our rabbi won't let you come to the synagogue with the rest of us, but here you are making jokes."

I let the bucket down, heard it splash down there, and then started pulling on the rope. "It's an adventure, Deborah."

"What do you mean, 'an adventure'?"

Hauling the full bucket up, I said, "We are striking out on our own into uncharted waters. Jesus is the captain of our ship, so we are unafraid."

For the first time ever, I believe I had Deborah's undivided attention. I lifted the bucket and poured the water into my pot. Then I dropped the bucket down the well again.

"Is your savta teaching you? I imagine you're the only one, right?"

"Yes," I said as I started tugging on the tight rope again.

She moved over beside me and (surprise!) helped me with it. Her hands looked so delicate holding the rough rope. I noticed how prettily her brows arched over her dark eyes as she turned to me and said, "She is a wonderful teacher. When I heard her announce school again, I almost clapped! But now I'm forbidden to go." Her pink lips were very close to pouting. *Like a two-year-old*, I thought.

"Abba said he will hire me a teacher from Jerusalem. Instead, I told him I have a plan." She waited until I poured the full bucket into my pot. When I looked back up toward her, she said, "What if I could persuade your savta to teach without mentioning Jesus of Nazareth? Then, just maybe, the rabbi would allow me to attend her school. When I told my abba my plan, he said, 'It's possible.'"

"It's *im*possible! She would never agree to that—not after what He's done for her!"

Maybe I sounded mad, and maybe I was! I picked up my full water pot, and said, "In our school, Jesus will have the honor He deserves, Deborah. You are welcome to come, but that is how it will always be."

She stared at me with her mouth hanging open. Right then, beautiful Deborah didn't strike me as beautiful at all. I left for home.

CHAPTER SIXTEEN
THE FISHING LESSON

WHAT a surprise I had when Savta dismissed me from school Thursday! As I stepped outside of Room Beth, I heard a familiar voice say, "Lanee, you're here!"

Could it be? Across the courtyard, for the first time since our joyful time at the feast, came Ben, his tan face lit up with a happy smile.

"Hello, Ben," I called with my heart thumping. "Yes, this room is my classroom now."

He walked through the flowers to me. The unruly thatch of hair that usually fell into his eyes was shorter. He had on a dark tunic of linen with a leather belt loosely riding his hips. Coming closer, I saw in his eyes how delighted he was to see me.

How I'd missed him, too, but now *he is here! Oh, Ben, you're here!*

All at once, I had a most disturbing thought. *Does he know we've been banned from the synagogue?* I tried to see by his expression as he drew closer. All I saw was tender gladness on the dearest of all faces.

"Your classroom?" he said as he reached me. "Oh ... praise the LORD! I'll be working for Yosef beginning this evening. I'll get to see you here!" He stood before me, looking at my hair, my eyes, my lips, and I felt my upturned face heating up. "I don't have to start work yet, so may I walk you home?"

I nodded, though I didn't know if Eema and Abba would approve. It was my first invitation.

He took my hand, and we began walking toward my house. As we passed the stable yard, he said, "Did you know I went to Jerusalem for the feast of Pentecost? We took a long side trip to Caesarea afterwards to see my abba's folks. They are in their eighties and aren't well. We just returned to Arbela yesterday."

That explained why I hadn't seen him at any Sabbath services. It could be he *hadn't* heard about us. Glancing over at his joyous face, I surely didn't want to tell him.

"Did you go to Jerusalem for Pentecost, too?" he asked. "I didn't see you, though I looked for you everywhere."

So much had happened I didn't know where to start. His hand felt cool and strong around mine. I gazed down the path that cut through the sycamore trees toward my house. Under their spreading limbs and wide green leaves, it seemed we were strolling through a natural temple. The dappled sunlight danced over Ben's arms and chest. He bent his head, seeking my eyes.

So *much* had happened—where did I start? Suddenly I remembered Savta.

"I went to the feast, Ben, but we were called back to my savta. She was dying. But, you know what? Jesus healed her, and she is my teacher once more!" I felt the joy of it all over again.

"*Jesus* healed her?" he asked with a puzzled look. "Isn't He dead? Or isn't He raised up and gone? Lanee, what are you talking about?"

I tried to explain. "Jesus is in Heaven, Ben, but He promised if we would believe in Him, we would do greater things than He did while He was here. When Savta was sick, we prayed for her, and finally she prayed for herself. Then Jesus saved her and healed her!"

We continued a few more steps then Ben stopped and turned toward me, "I've been thinking much about this. If Jesus *is* the Son of God, why, He can do anything! Even what you said—heal your savta from Heaven."

"That's exactly what he did, Ben! In fact, He did it last week."

I could tell by the way he looked down as we walked that he was wrestling with it. When he spoke again, he seemed to be feeling after the right words.

"I *am* interested in Jesus, but I can't say I love Him. You love Him, Lanee, and are loyal to Him. I like to hear about His works, but why should I love Him? Does He need me to love Him?"

Lord, I don't know what to tell him.

We were almost out of the trees near my house. He let go of my hand and said, "I'd better turn back here. Yosef will soon be ready for me to help him in the kitchen. I'll try to meet you after school tomorrow." He started back a ways then turned and saw me still looking. He grinned at me and waved, calling, "Shalom, Lanee!"

I walked into the house up on a cloud again. *Oh, Ben.*

The next morning was Friday, the last school day before the Sabbath. Savta started the day out saying, "You've really been working hard every day, Lanee. Would you like to do something different this afternoon?"

"Oh, yes. What is it, Savta?"

"Yosef wants to take us on a fishing lesson."

I had fished some with Abba from the shore, but Yosef

was going to take us out on one of his boats. I couldn't wait!

Finally afternoon came. We walked around the back of the inn to the dock where Yosef tied his boats. He was already there loading a wad of net into the back of one. Then I saw Ben heading from the inn toward us.

Yosef saw me looking and explained. "I've asked Benjamin to come along and help us with the rowing." He raised his voice, "Did you bring the food pouch?" Ben held it up. Yosef grinned at Savta and me and said, "We might get a little hungry before we come back in." I was feeling more and more excited about this fishing lesson by the minute.

First Yosef escorted Savta to the bow of the small boat, then told Ben and me to sit in the middle beside each other. He pushed off from the shore and got in behind us. Ben grabbed the handle of the oar on his side, and I followed his lead, dipping my oar into the still water.

When his dark eyes turned toward me, all I could think was, am I able to use this oar? I held it out over the water then dug down deep. Oh no, I could barely pull it! I knew that wasn't right. I brought it up shallow. Then I jerked hard, and it flew out of the water spraying Ben and me all over. His eyes looked tickled, but he didn't laugh. He waited until I got my oar back in the water then began again. I tried to copy him. At last, I was getting it. It felt good to pull my oar in time with his.

We rowed out from the shore toward the middle of the vast lake. My arms were protesting by then.

Yosef spoke directions to us, "Pick up your oar, Lanee, so Ben can turn us. Now pull together again. He showed Ben how to allow for my weaker rowing. When he could see we both were tiring, he said, "Pull up your paddles and rest a while."

The gliding craft gave us a peaceful ride. In front, Savta closed her eyes and seemed to be savoring the caress of the air against her face. Ben sat still beside me, relaxing his arms. I ventured a peek at him. Our eyes met and his curving lips turned up a little more into a soft smile. I gave him one back.

"You two rested enough?" Yosef asked behind us.

We picked up our oars and pulled hard again. The lake water's fishy smell rose up around us. Before we needed another rest, we were there—the place Yosef called his secret spot. "Stop rowing, and lift your oars quietly," he instructed in a low voice. We did. Yosef picked up the wad of net lying between his feet. He whispered, "Watch carefully."

He tied the rope around his arm, put a piece of the net edge in his mouth, and shook the net loose from its wadded condition. It was circular. He picked up a section of the bottom of the net, held it out, twisted his body around, and whirled quickly back toward the water. With a flick of his wrist, out flew the net in a perfect floating circle. It sank suddenly when it hit the water.

Yosef let it settle then he gave some short tugs on the rope. "That's to close the net," he said louder and then he began to pull it up hand over hand. Then he wasn't quiet at all, but cried, "Whoa Benjamin! Step back here and help me!" Ben stepped over the seat immediately and grabbed onto the rope. They hauled up the net with straining arms. When Yosef shook the rope loose, thirty fish flopped on the bottom of the boat! He must have surprised a whole school of musht. A few of the striped silver fish were as long as my forearm.

Savta laughed, and I squealed—I'd never seen such a thing!

Yosef and Ben picked up the fish and threw them in the hold up near Savta. One got away, which she caught with a practiced hand and threw it in after the others. I wasn't so sure about handling the wildly flopping things—their fins looked sharp!

Yosef gave the net to Ben. He placed his hands over Ben's, showing him the holding techniques, twisting with him, and swinging his arm out over the lake with Ben's. Out went the net and only half opened. Ben practiced a few throws by himself, and soon with Yosef's advice, had the knack of it. Then Yosef helped me as he had Ben. We laughed at my throws, until I finally cast it out, and the net bloomed out over the water like a pretty brown flower. I guess we'd scared the fish away with all our noisy practicing, for I didn't pull any up.

We rowed over to another of Yosef's favorite spots. "All right, Benjamin, it's your turn," Yosef whispered. He came up beside me to give Ben plenty of room. Ben cast the net out not quite perfectly. After it sank, he gave the short tugs on the rope then began to haul it up.

"Come on, Lanee, help me!" I moved quickly when I saw his face getting red. We heaved as hard as we could, and no wonder—when we got the net to the surface it was crammed full of fish! Ben and I laughed aloud as we strained to pull them up into the boat. Now we must have caught more than fifty fish!

We rested while Yosef and Savta stowed the fish. Then Yosef said, "One more spot." We picked up our oars and rowed to the new place he pointed out. He motioned us to lift our oars and said softly, "Lanee, it's your turn."

I felt nervous, and that's probably why my first cast didn't open. I quickly gathered it back in and tried again. This time the net opened perfectly. I watched it sink, tugged the net closed, and pulled. The weight I felt on the rope made me know I had something! Ben came back and helped me haul up another net full of musht. What a thrill! I picked them up this time placing my hand over the top fin as Savta did. Now our storage hold was full.

"Let's row over to that outcropping of rocks," Yosef said.

When we reached the shore, we got out and saw it was some kind of camping spot. There were the remains of a fire under an iron grill in the trampled grass.

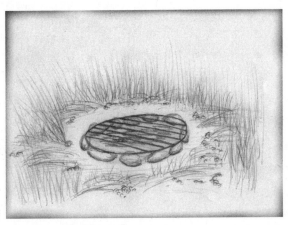

"Benjamin, bring me the food pouch. Rose and Lanee, will you pick out four of the nicest fish?" He began gathering wood from under the trees growing farther back from the shore. He threw it into a pile then pulled something wrapped in leather out of the bulging food pouch. When he unwrapped the layers of leather, I saw it was a small clay pot with a handle that was full of hot coals. He set the pot on the ground and stuck little sticks in it. As the fire caught, he added wood.

He handed us some knives from the pouch, and we went

down to the shore to clean our fish. Yosef laid them on the grill, pulling spices out of the pouch to season them. We sat on the flattened grass watching the fire and talking while the fish cooked. How delicious those fresh-caught musht smelled!

When he served up a hot fish on each of our thin metal plates, we were more than ready to eat. We moved away from the fire and sat down under a large oak. Smiling, Yosef offered his hands to Ben and me, and nodded to Savta. She took our other hands and bowed her head, "Thank you, dear Lord for the fish and for our children," she prayed, "Bless our food and them, in Jesus' name, Amen."

We didn't just have fish to eat. Yosef had brought flat dark bread and a skin full of grape juice. That fish was cooked just the way I liked it—crispy outside with firm white flakes within.

After we finished, Yosef lay back on the grass and gazed up through the oak canopy into the azure sky. "Would you like to know why I brought you to this spot?"

I recognized Yosef's story-telling voice. "Yes, Yosef, please."

Ben and Savta leaned contentedly against the oak trunk and I sat across from Yosef.

"I've had a strong yearning to come here ever since we returned from Jerusalem. There I heard Simon Peter talk about the time he met Jesus after He'd risen from the dead. It was by the shore of our Sea of Galilee. "

Yosef rolled over on his side facing the shore. He propped his grizzled head on his strong brown arm, and continued, "When the opportunity came, I asked him privately just where they were that day. We both know this lake like the backs of our hands. He pointed me here."

Yosef sat up and looked around with an expression of

awe on his aged face, "Probably the last time that grill was used, Jesus used it to cook fish and bread for His disciples. Though I have come here hundreds of times over the years, now Jesus has made it a holy place for me."

I glanced at Ben. With a puzzled look, he brushed his hair back off his forehead and asked, "Uh, Yosef, what are you saying? Do *you* love Jesus?"

Yosef's sober face burst into that smile he'd found on the road to Jerusalem. He turned and said, "Yes, Benjamin ben Jacob, I do love Him—and with all my heart!"

CHAPTER SEVENTEEN

DAVID AND EEMA LIRA COME

YOSEF decided I'd had enough rowing for one day. So I sat beside Savta in the bow of the boat, while he helped Ben get us home. Ben was silent the whole trip. As we got close to the dock, I saw Abba there waiting with a big barrel ready to receive our fish.

"Yosef, do you always catch this many fish?" I asked.

He laughed and said, "I can't lie—often I do. Don't tell anyone about my secret holes."

Abba caught the rope Ben threw out, and pulled us to the bank. "Did she catch any, Yosef?" he asked as I stepped out of the boat into his hug.

"We *all* did, Jonathan. Well, except Rose. You know, I didn't even offer you a chance at it, Rose."

Savta waved him off, saying, "I loved watching as much as trying it myself. Next time, Yosef."

Abba and Ben got busy throwing the fish from the hold into the barrel.

"Now's when the fun starts, Lanee! We get to clean all these nice fish," Yosef said, and then headed toward the inn to get more knives and clean pans.

Not far from the dock, a fish-cleaning table stood right at the lakeshore. Abba and Ben carried the barrel of fish over, and all of us pitched in to get them cleaned. We relived the

147

fishing lesson as we scaled and removed heads and entrails. The flies zoomed in for their supper. Ben seemed very engrossed in his fish scaling.

I chattered away. "On one of my casts, Abba, I almost flew right out of the boat along with the net."

We all laughed. I saw Ben smile, but he stayed well outside of the fun. I wondered what he was thinking.

When the last fish was in the briny water, Yosef thanked us all. We washed up in the lake then Abba, Savta, and I left for home. Soon the sun would set and the Sabbath would begin. Though Ben lived in the opposite direction, he caught up with us and asked, "Sir, may I walk Lanee home?"

Abba studied his serious face then nodded. He and Savta went ahead, leaving Ben and me alone.

We walked a ways without saying anything. He looked straight ahead, and I kept checking to see if he was turning my way. I can't remember him ever being this somber. Even the natural curl of his lip was straight.

I decided to ask him. "Ben, is something bothering you?"

"Look, Lanee, how can I love Jesus? I'm a man. It was all right for you to love Him—you're a girl—but I don't know *how* to love Him!" He quieted down for a few steps then he said, "When Yosef told me *he* loved Him with all his heart, I began to feel … well … left out. But as I consider loving Him, I get stuck on this problem—how *can* I love another man? It just doesn't feel right!

"Wait a minute, Ben. My abba loves Jesus. Is it possible that he could help you?"

"Well … yes, maybe. I am so confused!"

We walked on in silence. Then I ventured, "When we get

148

to the house, do you want to talk to Abba? Sometimes I don't understand things, but when I talk to him he helps me."

"I guess I'd better try. Thanks, Lanee." Ben almost took my hand then drew his back. "I'm sorry, Lanee, my hands smell awful."

"I'm already covered in it, so a little more won't hurt." I said with a laugh. I held out my hand and he took it.

The sun was just going down when we reached my house. The sound of voices coming from the courtyard told me we had company.

Abba called to me, "Lanee! Lanee! Guess who's here?" Just then, David bolted out of the door, grabbed me up in his arms, and swung me around!

"Oh, David! David! You're here!" How surprised and pleased I was to see him again. My brother David, with his dark curls and handsome face. "Is Eema Lira here, too?" I cried, as he let me down.

Smiling, she emerged from the door and caught me up in her arms. "Oh, Lanee, it is wonderful to see you again!"

Then I remembered Ben. He looked at me. He looked at David. Then he looked down at his feet. I think he was mad.

"Oh, David and Eema Lira, I want you to meet Benjamin ben Jacob, my dear friend."

They both turned to him with a glad smile.

"It's good to meet you, but I need to get home. Goodbye, Lanee."

CHAPTER EIGHTEEN

CHURCH AT THE INN

IT was our first Sabbath outside of the synagogue. Abba took the opportunity to study the Scriptures. He had borrowed Yosef's scroll of the Prophet Isaiah, searching it for references to the Messiah. With few exceptions, the adults in our village believed in the Word of God. Perhaps, as Yosef had come to believe in Jesus through seeing Him in prophecies, so could others in the village.

The rest of us decided to spend time praying. The experience in the upper room at Pentecost had let us know God hears and answers earnest prayer. We gathered in the front room after the noon meal.

I asked, "Please pray for Ben. Today he will learn we are not welcome in the synagogue, if he doesn't already know. Pray for God to give him wisdom." Though I didn't say it aloud, I thought, *and help him to understand about David.*

David's deep voice came from the low stool in the corner. "Please pray for Eema and me that we find a place to live and a job. Thank you for allowing us to stay with you, but as soon as possible, we would like to have our own place." He looked over at Eema Lira sitting comfortably on a large cushion near the open door. She nodded.

Eema and I were sharing the oak bench across from them. She asked with tears gathering in her brown eyes, "Please pray for our first church meeting tomorrow. Pray that Jesus will help our love for Him to grow even though

151

others do not believe."

When everyone knelt to pray, I let Eema have the bench. I grabbed a soft cushion and knelt down by the stairs. It felt good to pour my troubles out to Jesus. It felt restful. Perhaps I was learning the true purpose of the Sabbath at home on my knees.

Spending this queen of all days outside of the synagogue was different from any Sabbath I'd ever had. After our prayer time, the hours seemed empty. I wondered out to the courtyard looking for Nanny's kids. They were half-grown, knobby-kneed, and friendly. David came out and sat with me. He coaxed Whitey to him, offering her some raisins. Blackie came, too.

"They like you, David. At least they like that one hand of yours."

He laughed and looked over at me. "Maybe I should have held out some raisins to Ben yesterday. I don't think he was too glad to make my acquaintance." He paused, then asked, "You like him, don't you, Lanee?"

"Only since I was twelve."

David smiled his white-toothed smile with his chin in his hand and said, "I'm sorry for greeting you like I did. I've missed you so much that when I saw you, I couldn't help but hug you."

"And swing me around." I gave him a pointed look.

"That, too, Lanee," he said with a bigger grin. "I've never had a friend like you. In fact, Eema and I have never had friends like Yosef and your family." Then his eyes widened, "Oh, yes, Lanee, did you know Dod Ethan found us when he came back to Jerusalem? He told us Savta was better. Later he visited us again and brought us several changes of new clothes. He said the Lord laid it on his heart to do it! We sat with him and Dod Micah writing down more testimonies of the disciples."

David looked down at Whitey who was nudging his hand with her head. He smoothed down the wiry hair between her ears.

I couldn't help staring at my handsome friend. His black hair framed a fine face with the deepest blue eyes. He was wearing a well-fitting tunic made of soft brown linen. Again, I felt awed by his beauty. *This must be what it would be like to be friends with King David. And my David is surely every bit as kingly as our shepherd boy of old was.*

Looking back at me over Whitey's head, he said, "Even though there were many other believers in Jerusalem, our hearts were on coming to Arbela to be with all of you."

"How *did* you come, David?"

"One of the brothers at the upper room said he was going back home to Capernaum, and would someone like to travel with him with his livestock? He and his wife were grateful for us coming along with them as far as Arbela. We offered to continue on to Capernaum, but he said he could easily handle those few miles alone."

"I'm so glad you're here, for I've missed you, too."

"Listen, Lanee, don't worry about Ben. If the Lord will give me a chance, I'll straighten his thinking out about you and me. I have a reputation to uphold, remember. David to the rescue!"

He smiled his gorgeous smile, and I began to feel better about Ben. Who could resist such a friend?

~~~

The bright summer sunshine ushered in the first day of the week and our first church service at the inn. We arrived early enough to arrange the Window Room into rows of seats facing the pulpit Abba had built. Yosef invited his staff of maids, cooks, and stable hands to attend the service.

Eema, Savta, and I sat on the first row with David and Eema Lira. Yosef and his staff sat in the row behind us. I heard someone clear his throat back there and I knew Ben had come. *Jesus will you help Ben and me?* I prayed, as I fought the urge to turn and look at him.

Abba stepped behind the pulpit and started the service. "There has never been a church in Arbela. Jesus told Peter when he acknowledged Him as the Christ, 'Upon this rock I will build my church, and the gates of hell shall not prevail against it.' We are at its beginning. Let's pray together, dear brothers and sisters, that God will help us be both joyful and strong for Him!"

Abba motioned with his strong calloused hands for us to stand. We rose up and prayed, sensing the greatness of the moment. I forgot about Ben and just prayed, asking Jesus for what Abba wanted us to be—a joyful church, a strong church!

Suddenly the Holy Ghost came down in our midst, falling on all of us believers. We spoke in those strange tongues, allowing the power of the Holy Ghost to have His way. Again, I felt the joy of God being right inside of me, causing me to speak words I didn't even know.

When the Spirit lifted, we looked around, and all the staff had left, except Ben.

Abba spoke again from the pulpit, "We must understand that no one has ever seen the moving of the Holy Ghost before in our village. The staff running away is just the beginning of how people will react to the manifestation of the Holy Ghost power. It will be misunderstood, feared, laughed at, and scorned. But Jesus sent us our Comforter, and we will always yield to Him to comfort, lead, assure, and even protect us."

Then Abba asked David and Eema Lira to sing the worship song they had practiced at home.

> "Dear Jesus, we are your hands,
> For yours were scarred for us;
> Dear Savior, we are your feet,
> For yours were marred for us;
> Surely as you gave your all,
> We offer our all to you."

Their voices blended in sweet harmony; their faces were lit with the joy of the Lord. After they sang it a few times, we joined in. Then I heard a new voice singing behind me, low and sad, almost changing the song's sound to a minor key. It was Ben.

Abba began his talk. "In the prophet Isaiah's writings, he foretells that 'a virgin shall conceive and bear a son, and shall call his name, Immanuel.' Most of us had the privilege to meet Mary, Jesus' eema, in the upper room at Pentecost. She said the angel Gabriel had visited her when she was a young virgin and proclaimed that Jesus would be born of her. She testified that He truly is God's Son." Abba paused, his face rapt with the truth he spoke. "When I read these words, yesterday, I discovered Isaiah said Mary would call

Him, 'Immanuel.' Do you know what *Immanuel* means? It means *God with us.*"

I glanced over at Savta. She saw me and reached for my hand.

Abba continued, "Out on the fields of Arbela, we saw Him healing the sick—not a few, but hundreds were healed! God was with us! We also heard of His power to walk on the water of this lake right behind us. Surely, God *has* been with us! But, listen to what I believe the Holy Ghost revealed to me about His name, Immanuel. He means to be *with us:* with you, with me, and with everyone who wants Him. That's His very name; it is so much what He is!"

Abba's tears began rolling down his cheeks. He raised his hands and cried out, "Oh Immanuel, my Jesus, how blessed I am to have you in my life!"

Abba's praise got us all up on our feet, praising the Lord. *Jesus, thank you, my Immanuel! I've been learning every day how good it is to have you with me!*

When we quieted, Abba spoke to Yosef, "Will you finish our first church service with a prayer, dear friend?"

At first, he seemed surprised, but then he gave Abba a pleased smile. He bowed his gray head over two gnarled hands and prayed, "Jesus, continue to bless us with your presence and your love. Lead us, Holy Ghost, and comfort us. Thank you, our Father, for so great salvation. In Jesus' name, Amen."

It just seemed natural to hug Eema, Eema Lira, and Savta after the prayer. Abba and Yosef hugged each other then they hugged David. I saw Abba put his arm around Ben's shoulders and greet him kindly. Then we began rearranging the dining room, for soon hungry travelers would arrive for their noon meal.

Ben and I met at one of the tables and we carried it over to the corner. I smiled into his dark eyes, but then was puzzled by the look he gave me. He seemed … *awestruck!*

I didn't have a chance to question him, for just then Yosef came out of the kitchen exclaiming, "Not only have the staff left the meeting—some of them have quit their jobs!" He suddenly turned to David, "Son, can you and your eema help me today?" Then to Eema Lira, "I need your help in the kitchen, Lira—and David, can you serve and help with the dishes?"

David looking quite amazed, said, "Yes sir, I can!" He looked at his eema and they both broke out into wide grins.

"Thank you, Lord," Yosef said. "Come, I'll show you around in the kitchen, Lira. Benjamin, show David where the tablecloths and napkins are."

Satisfied that Yosef had enough help, Eema and I walked Savta home. Abba, who had always worked on Sunday, stayed to manage the operation of the inn as usual. How *unusual* this Sunday felt to me—special and set apart for the Lord. And today, Abba had become much more than the manager of the inn. He had entered in to a new calling—the leader of our church.

Then I thought of the exciting turn things had taken. *Ben and David are working together right now, Lord. That's amazing! And oh, I believe you are right in the middle of this, my Immanuel!*

CHAPTER NINETEEN

THE HOLY GHOST AND THE GIRLS

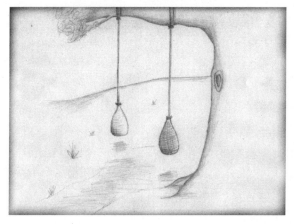

F OR the first time since we'd started school, I noticed
how empty our classroom really was. *I wish the other
girls were here!* I hadn't seen Sarah or Elisabeth
since our last Sabbath at the synagogue. We'd always
known each other, and it seemed strange not to see them
anymore. I wondered what they were doing about school.
Though Deborah's abba and perhaps Sarah's could afford
to hire tutors, I knew Elisabeth's and Misha's couldn't.

After school, I asked Eema, "May I go to the playground?"
She said yes, so I ran out into the hot afternoon sun toward
the village playground, hoping I'd at least see Elisabeth there.

When I arrived, the sack swings in the high trees were
hanging still. I looked farther toward the oaks so ancient my

abba had climbed on them when he was a boy. It was our old meeting spot—and there they were! Sarah was perched on the lowest limb of our favorite oak, making it bounce. Elisabeth and Misha were on a higher limb laughing as they showered her head with leaves. In the comfortable seat formed by the tree's upraised roots sat Deborah, leaning against its massive trunk. She noticed me and pointed.

Suddenly it seemed just like many other summers—when we finished our chores, we'd meet there to climb, swing, and mostly talk.

"Hey, Lanee! Come over!" Elisabeth yelled. I saw her long dark braids hanging over her shoulders.

Sarah and Deborah looked at each other and frowned as I walked closer. Elisabeth climbed out of the tree and ran to meet me. "I've been missing you," she said and gave me quick hug.

"I missed you, too." We walked together toward the others.

"Hello, Misha!" I called, smiling up at her.

When Elisabeth left, she had stretched full length along the limb. With her sandy hair trailing down, she smiled back at me. Then I said, "Hello, Deborah. Hello Sarah." They just looked at me.

Elisabeth asked, "Want to swing, Lanee?"

"Sure!" We two went flying to the sack swings, flipping off our sandals on the run. We grabbed the swings and pulled them back, then ran as fast as we could and jumped on almost at the same time.

"Are you going to school?" I asked after I caught my breath. We leaned out and in to keep the swings flying high.

"No, we don't have a teacher, yet. Is your savta teaching you?"

"Yes. It's been really fun *and* hard work." I leaned back, letting my hair fly out behind me. "Savta is teaching me such interesting things about our Jewish history. Then she requires me to write a report on what I've learned. It's hard, but I'm learning a lot! She even took me on a fishing lesson, Elisabeth—out in a boat on the lake. You should have been there! I wish you were in school with me."

"I can't," She said sadly. "My abba says he doesn't agree with the rabbi about the school, but we can't go against him."

All was quiet then but the creaking of the ropes. When I glanced over my shoulder at the giant oak, I saw Sarah, Deborah, and Misha heading our way. By the look on Sarah's face, I knew she wasn't coming to tell me how much she'd missed me. *Jesus, help me!*

Drawing near, Sarah said, "Lanee, stop for a minute. We want to ask you a question."

I quit leaning and let the swing slow down.

"We've heard something about you, and we'd like to ask you if it is true."

I let the swing stop and jumped down. "What is it?"

This time it was Deborah who spoke. "We heard that you sometimes start speaking gibberish, and your whole family does, too. And that you believe *God* is causing you to do it. Is that true?"

I could feel my face heating up. I walked away to where my sandals were, brushed off my feet, and put them back on. I had no idea how to answer her. *Lord, help me.*

Then Misha reported, "My Dodah Mary worked for Mar

161

Yosef. She said he gave them a break from work just to sit in the dining room for what he called *church*. She was glad to sit down instead of sweeping. But when she saw and heard all of you, it scared her so badly she quit and went home. She said, 'Everyone had lost their minds, saying things no one else could understand.' She said even Mar Yosef was doing it, and that's why she quit—she didn't want to work for a madman."

I didn't know what to say. I hated that my face was flushed.

Deborah's beautiful eyes bore into mine. I looked at Sarah's freckled face. She knew I was squirming, but still she fixed her green eyes on me and scowled.

That did it! How many times had we squared off like this over who was going to be first, or whose turn it was next? My promise that Jesus gave me was real, and I would not let Sarah and Deborah, or anyone else, scorn it!

"All right, I'll tell you about it, but first let's go sit down." I led them to the grassy spot underneath our oak. We sat in a circle as we had done many times in the past. But today, I didn't feel like a friend.

"Do you really want to know what's happening? Or do you just want to make light of it?" I asked. "If that's the case, I won't tell you." I looked each of them in the eyes, hoping to find a spark of true interest. None of them answered my question.

Then Elisabeth said, "Lanee, it *sounds* insane, but I know you are not insane. So, will you tell us?"

Sarah and company had focused their eyes on the grass. They didn't want me to see what was in them. Suddenly it didn't matter what they thought. I wanted to tell them. *It's you, isn't it, Jesus?*

I gazed into Elisabeth's soft brown eyes and began, "Jesus gave His followers a promise when He went back up to Heaven. He promised to send us another Comforter. When we went to Jerusalem for the feast of Pentecost, we were with His disciples in a large upper room when God sent the promise. There were one hundred and twenty of us. Jesus' eema was there, too."

As I unfolded the beautiful memory, my eyes rose above Elisabeth's head to the blue shimmering sky. "On the day of Pentecost, there suddenly came a rushing mighty wind blowing through the room. At that moment, I opened my mouth and out came words I did not understand. All around me, the others were doing the same. There were tongues of fire on everyone's heads, but we weren't burned. Peter, Jesus main disciple, said it was the Holy Ghost that Jesus sent. Since then, every time He comes down upon us the same thing happens—we speak in a language we don't understand."

I turned my eyes back on the girls, finding all four of them staring at me.

"Do it now," Sarah said.

"Didn't you hear me, Sarah? It isn't me; it is only when the Holy Ghost comes upon me."

"Why?" Deborah asked with that spark of interest now in her eyes.

"I believe it is to show that He is with us. When I speak the strange words, I know He is speaking through me. He's that close!"

Elisabeth asked quietly, "Is it scary?"

"No, it's wonderful. I have always wanted to be close to

God, but I didn't know how. Now it feels as if He has moved right inside me."

They didn't say anything more, so I said, "Your dodah should come back and try to understand about the Holy Ghost, Misha. When He lit on Jesus' head at the Jordan River, it was in the form of a harmless little dove." I got up and brushed off my skirt. "I'd better go now. Maybe I'll see you again tomorrow."

I left, feeling their stares boring into my back. When I got out of their sight, I jumped up and down with joy, and ran as fast as I could, crying out in my loudest whisper, "Oh, thank you, Jesus!"

CHAPTER TWENTY

BEAUTY AND BEN

I T turned out to be a blessing that Misha's dodah and the
others quit the inn after our church service. Yosef didn't
just use David and Eema Lira that day, but he hired them
to fill their spots. And after just a week, the Lord showed
He had something even better planned for David.

On Monday, Daniel ben Judah, Deborah's abba, stopped in
at the inn for his noon meal. David was his server. When Mar
Daniel finished his meal, he sought out Yosef, then walked
up to David and offered him a job on his sprawling farm.

"He's giving me a better wage than I have ever earned!"
David exclaimed, telling us about it that night. Even though
Yosef needed David, he had agreed to release David from
his job at the inn. He knew it was a better opportunity
for him.

The next day David and his eema went looking for a house. They came back with good news—they'd found a small house on the street near the well and could move in right away.

Then on Wednesday, David went to Daniel ben Judah's farm to start his job. I heard him calling from the road late that afternoon, "Oh, Lanee, where are you?"

I went to the front door. "What did he have you doing, David?" I asked, laughing at the white teeth and eyes shining out of the dirty face.

"I'm learning to harvest figs. The grove is dry and dusty. Do I look that bad?"

I thought, *No, Mar Dirty Face, not nearly as bad as I did when you first laid eyes on me—face down in stable muck!*

"How could you?" I said smiling.

He looked puzzled at my words, then said, "Mar Judah's fig trees are right by the lake. I guess I'll wade in for a bath tomorrow before I come home."

"Sit down and rest, David, and tell me how you like it." I sat under the sycamore tree and he sat beside me. Suddenly he stretched himself out on the grass with a great sigh.

"It's hard work! Even my bones feel tired." He turned over on his stomach, looking at me with his head propped on his hands. "But, I really like being outside, even if it *is* broiling hot. I remember working for the blacksmith. How hot that place was, and Yosef's kitchen, too. I think I'm going to enjoy the outdoors work for a change. Jesus is so good to me!"

He dropped his head on his dirty arms. The gentle breeze under the tree ruffled his curly hair. He might have dropped off to sleep. I looked away and smoothed the skirt of my tunic, thinking how good Jesus was to me, too.

"Lanee." He said with his face still resting on his arms.

"Yes?"

He raised his head up to look at me, "Before I head home, I wanted to ask you if you've seen Ben."

"Not since both of us saw him last Sunday at church." I said. I remembered Ben was the quiet watcher in the background as we worshiped the Lord. I wanted to talk to him afterwards, but he went right back to work.

David sat up to look me in the eyes, "We worked together all last week, and I see why you like him, Lanee. He works like he loves it, and when he's through with his work, he jumps in to help someone else with theirs."

I looked away toward the road, thinking of Ben.

"One night we were washing dishes together," said David, "and I told him how we met. I even told him about the upper room and the Holy Ghost coming down on all of us."

"Oh my, David, what did he say?"

"He didn't say anything—just looked at me with those dark troubled eyes of his. His face was so glum. We finished the dishes without talking anymore. Then I said, 'Ben, you don't need to worry about Lanee and me. We're just friends.'

"He answered me, 'I know that … now.'

"So I said, 'Then what did I say that bothered you?'

"At first, I thought he wasn't going to answer me. I grabbed the broom and started sweeping. Next thing I know, his hand is on my arm stopping the broom. He looks me straight in the eye and says, 'I feel like I'm on the outside looking in. I can't find the door to get inside with you and with Lanee

… and with Jesus.'"

I felt tears for Ben spring up into my eyes.

David said, "All of a sudden, something happened in my heart—it was like a bucket of faith turned over and soaked me good, down deep! Grinning into his sad face, I said, 'Oh, you will, Ben, oh, how you will!' Though he was puzzled, he couldn't help it, he smiled back at me."

David stood up, just as dirty, but looking refreshed. He reached for my hand to pull me up. "See, Lanee, I told you I would fix it, though it did take some help from the Lord to get him to smile. Now, I'd better get going. Eema will be looking for me. Shalom!"

That night I couldn't sleep. Out on the rooftop, I looked to the great Friend who had helped me with Ben before. *Jesus, I know if Ben could really know you, he would love you. Will you help him, Lord? you're the only one who can help him, Jesus. Please do.*

I leaned on the half wall praying until I was released from the fear and heaviness I felt for Ben. Then I dropped on my mat and slept.

Savta worked me hard the following day at school. She assigned me many computations in mathematics. I had to double and triple a recipe for goat stew, and even figure out how much wood I'd need to build a shed for Nanny and the kids. Then there were number problems to solve.

I also was working on a project I'd started last week—writing an essay on the prophecies of the Messiah in the Book of Isaiah. Since the first week of school, we had been digging in the Scriptures, unearthing all the prophets' foretelling of His coming. Savta and I were thrilled daily at how Jesus' life matched these completely. Here's an example: Though Mary, Jesus' eema, was from Nazareth, she testified that Jesus was born in Bethlehem. His birth there fulfilled the prophet Micah's words—*But thou Bethlehem Ephratah, though thou be little among the thousands of Judah, yet out of thee shall he come forth unto me that is to be the ruler of Israel.*

It was time for school to end for the day. I put away my work, prayed with Savta, and gave her a hug and a kiss. Stepping outside of Room Beth, I thought, *I wonder where Abba is? Maybe I'll say hello before I head home.* After I checked the stable, I walked around the inn, keeping my eyes open for Ben, too.

"Lanee! How was school?" It was Eema Lira, calling from the lakeshore.

I strolled down to the fish-cleaning table, where she was working. "Great, Eema Lira. I'm learning more about Jesus every day. Would you like some help?"

"You'll smell like a fish. Are you all right with that?"

I picked up the extra knife and began scaling a large shiny musht. "Who caught these?"

"Benjamin did. Yosef sends him out most early mornings to catch us fresh ones for the kitchen."

I enjoyed picturing him in the boat alone, watching the net fly out over the water in the foggy pink morning light. *He must have gotten good at it.*

Just then, Ben came up behind us, and asked, "Lira, may I borrow Lanee from you? Her abba wants me to show her the new boat Yosef bought."

Eema Lira nodded and said, "Thanks, Lanee. Go ahead, and I'll see you later." She gave me her pretty smile then said, "Your eema asked us to eat with you again tonight."

I went to the shore and washed my hands, watching the scales float away in the brownish water. I dried them on the skirt of my tunic, and looked up into Ben's eyes.

He led the way to the dock where a sleek new boat was tied. It was built of tawny polished lumber fitted with brass oarlocks that shone in the afternoon sun. Two smooth oars lay in its bottom. The builder had designed it with a seat up front, then one for the oarsman, and a large box built into the stern for the catch. The lid of the hold displayed hinges, and a hook and loop of shiny brass.

"Isn't she a beauty, Lanee?" He stepped inside and ran his hand along the polished beam. "It's fir wood. I took her out this morning and she handles easily with one person rowing. Yosef said he's going to call her Beauty. The man who built her is coming to paint the name on tomorrow."

Ben brushed his hair back then picked up one of the oars. "I've got the knack of casting the net, girl! When I get out on the water, I call to the thousands of musht out here, 'Watch out, fish, Benjamin the dreaded fisherman is coming after you!' Though I quiet down when I get near the good spots."

He jumped out and stood near me. "You want to take a ride in her? I'll row, and you can just enjoy it."

"Maybe I'd better check with Abba, Ben."

"Don't worry, Lanee, I've already cleared it with him."

"Then, yes, I'd love to ride in Beauty."

He offered me his hand, and I stepped carefully into the boat. When I sat down on the bench in the bow, the smell of the water and the grassy reeds rose up around me. Ben got in and untied the boat then pushed her off with an oar,

170

He rowed easily toward the middle of the lake.

"You could handle her yourself. Want to try?"

I shook my head, content to lean back and enjoy our glide over the water. I heard a fish flop and spotted the swirling whirlpool where he'd been.

> "Beauty on the water,
> Beauty on the sea,
> Beauty riding in the bow,
> Smiling back at me."

Ben sang it in a husky voice. He saw my surprise and laughed. "I couldn't help it, Lanee! How pretty you are, sitting there with the wind ruffling your hair."

Oh, Benjamin ben Jacob, how you have touched my heart!

I allowed myself the luxury of studying his features. The shining brown brush of hair fell over his smooth tan forehead. His lean jaw was almost covered by a neat beard. Below the Jewish curve of his nose, his smooth lips were curling toward a smile. As he rowed, strong brown arms and hands flexed muscles that strained the sleeves of his work tunic.

I studied his face and he studied mine. Our eyes met. Looking into his intelligent eyes, he allowed me a glimpse of his heart.

He said, "Do you mind if I stop rowing so we can talk?"

When he saw my smile, he pulled the oars out of the water. Beauty drifted on.

I remembered how confused he was the day he'd walked me home. "How are you doing, Ben?"

"I was just going to ask you the same thing. I didn't know until last Sabbath that the rabbi has forbidden your family and Yosef to attend the synagogue. You weren't there, so I asked my abba about you. He told me since you are believers in Jesus, Rabbi ben Tzadik has asked you not to come back."

Ben laid the oars down, and moved to my bench. He reached for my hand. "I can't believe he's done such a thing. Are you upset?" His strong hand felt good to me.

"I was at first, but then we started our church," I answered into his concerned eyes. "Except for being anxious over what you would think about us, I have been very blessed. What liberty we have in our church to worship Jesus! We never would have had that in the synagogue."

The boat rocked lightly. The sound of children playing by the lakeshore drifted across the water to us.

Then Ben said, "Lanee, when you and the others started speaking in those tongues in church Sunday, I was shocked just like the rest of the help. They left, but I couldn't, for something occurred to me that made the experience seem reasonable. We were there to worship God. Why would we expect *Him* always to do predictable human things? When I saw your joyful face speaking words I didn't understand, I thought, she's touching and being touched by God—how awesome! I'm glad your family has the church so you can worship like that." Ben stopped speaking and stared into my eyes for a long moment. "I'm not going back, Lanee. If you are not welcome in the synagogue, then neither am I!"

"But, Ben, unless you are a believer in Jesus, you are welcome there."

"I don't know *what else* I believe in, but I know I believe in you. And I'm not going where you are not welcome."

There was that feeling of belonging to each other again. Somehow, he had begun acknowledging it, too. His eyes told me his willingness was complete. Mine said it back.

Finally I spoke, "Ben, I need to get home and help Eema with supper."

He smiled and nodded, then moved back to his seat to row Beauty home. He pointed out a turtle to the right of us, and I spotted its crooked nose sticking up out of the water. "I see all kinds of creatures when I come out early in the morning. Maybe you could come with me one morning."

Soon he landed the boat, tied her up, and reached for my hand to help me out. "I'm needed in the kitchen today, Lanee," he said, "but, may I walk you home from school tomorrow?"

"Yes, I'd love that, Ben. Tell Abba how much I liked Beauty." We parted with a happy smile for each other.

When I got home, Eema told me she'd walk with me to the well. "I want to stop by Lira's on the way back."

The afternoon was steamy without the breeze from off the lake. Carrying our empty jugs down the dusty road, I had an urge to tell Eema how I felt about Ben. Eema's love for Abba had always been so real to me. *Is Ben my "Jonathan?"*

"How did you and Abba get together, Eema?" I started. "You never told me."

Eema seemed surprised. "Why, Lanee, I would love to tell you this today." She gave me a tender smile and said, "We were little children in our synagogue. He was the sweetest boy in the whole village. That's not just me saying it—he really was. His abba died when Jonathan was very young, but he had left Savta financially able to finish raising him and Ruth."

Eema shifted her clay jar to her other arm and continued, "I went to their house for school. One day when I was fifteen and Jonathan was eighteen, he told his eema he wanted to marry me and would she please talk to my parents. Lanee, he had never spoken to me alone. I didn't even know he liked me."

"Did you like him then, Eema?"

She blushed and said, "Oh, yes, I'd always liked him since we were children."

"Did he know?"

"After we married, he told me that's why he wanted to marry me. All he could remember from the time he was a boy was a girl with big brown eyes enjoying everything he said and did. He had grown up 'in the light of my loving eyes' and wanted to always have me with him."

When she didn't say any more, we walked on a few steps, and I said, "Eema, do you know how I feel about Ben?"

"Will you tell me?"

I took a deep breath and said, "Besides Jesus, he is all I think about." It was my turn to get red. "But I don't know if what I'm feeling is love like you and Abba have."

Eema placed her hand on my arm and stopped me, "Lanee, will you do something for me?"

"Yes, Eema, if I can."

"Will you talk to your abba about Ben?"

"I feel shy about it … but I'll try."

We walked on to the well, then stopped by Eema Lira's little house. She had just arrived home from working at the inn. The house was one-story with a lean-to out back. David had planted some wild windflowers in the yard that were struggling to grow. When she invited us in, we saw she didn't have many furnishings. Eema offered to make some cushions and mats to help decorate their new home. As we left the yard, she called back to Eema Lira, "Are you and David coming over for supper in a while?"

"We'll be there if the Lord is willing. And, Cilla, thank you."

We walked home carrying the full water jugs in silence. *Jesus, help me to talk to Abba. I don't even know how to start!* I thought, as I balanced the heavy sloshing jug on my head.

Supper was good that night. We ate as much as we wanted out of the great pot of lentils Eema served, along with wheat bread, olives, goat cheese, and ripe persimmons. Eema and Eema Lira discussed decorating her house as we ate. David and Abba talked about the Scriptures.

"Brother Jonathan, did King David know he would be the Messiah's great—many great—grandfather?"

I mostly ate and listened. And prayed. *Lord Jesus, will you please give me the courage to tell Abba about Ben?*

Both David and Eema Lira were tired after their workday, so they left right after helping with the dishes. I slipped the basket off its peg and went out to gather the day's eggs. My heart flip-flopped when I saw Abba feeding the chickens.

"Chick-chick-chick-chickoo! I know it's late, but come on chickens before you roost!" Abba threw barley all over the packed ground around the chicken pen. No problem with them coming—they ran from every direction! When Abba noticed me, he asked, "Did you have a good day, Lanee?"

I wasn't ready to talk about one part of my day, so I started out saying, "Eema and I went to the well together, and had a chance to talk."

He said, "Oh, yes? What did you girls talk about, if it's not a secret?"

"We talked about how you and Eema ... got together." When I said it, my face warmed up. I was standing beside the chicken coop and Abba was nearby in the yard. I saw my favorite hen fly awkwardly over the fence.

He threw a few more handfuls of grain before he said, "Well, that's interesting. I was just thinking about that today." He was smiling down at the chickens. "Did she tell you how I've always loved her? Did she tell you how shy I was, and how I could never talk to her after I was twelve years old? I talked to her sisters all the time, but got positively tongue-tied when Priscilla was around."

I tried to imagine my abba tongue-tied. I couldn't.

"Abba, she did tell me you always knew she liked you."

"Yes, I did. I think that was why my words were so bound up. One day when I was eighteen, I got tired of it. I decided to do something about Miss Cilla and me. I asked Savta to arrange our marriage." He looked at me and laughed. "We were married sixteen years ago today, my child."

"Oh! That's why you were thinking about it!" How dear this story was!

"Yes, my daughter, who is almost as old as your eema was when I married her." Then he chuckled some more.

Here goes ..."Uh, Abba ... do you ... do you like Ben?"

I couldn't face him, so I watched the chickens scratching at the ground for the last grains of barley. My hen pecked her way over to Abba's legs and swiveled her head up toward him as if to ask *any more?*

Abba's feet turned in my direction. *Bck-bock!* The hen flapped out of his way. When he reached me, he drew me into his arms. "Do *you* like Ben?" he almost whispered, resting his beard on my head.

"Yes, Abba, I really do."

"Now I will answer your question. I like him. But, Yonina, he is not saved. He has not accepted Jesus into his heart. I am not willing to give my daughter to a man who will not believe in our Savior. It would be too hard on you." He petted my hair gently. "We must pray for Ben, since it is he you have chosen. I know you well enough to know you will not be swayed from him—I remember your mother. But I also know that the Lord is in charge of it all, so we must ask for His help. Will you agree to do that, Lanee?"

I hugged him hard around his middle and said, "Oh, yes, Abba!"

CHAPTER TWENTY-ONE

THE BAPTIZING

I F it hadn't been for Savta, with all that was happening, I never would have been able to keep my mind on schoolwork. But she knew how to hold my interest.

"Would you like to learn about music, Lanee?" she asked on Monday. Since we'd started the church, music was a new love of mine. I think she'd noticed. "Yosef's father, our rabbi, sang the Psalms and accompanied himself on the harp," Savta reminisced. "Yosef still has his abba's harp, though I've never heard him play that wonderful instrument. Perhaps he will let us try our hands at it."

Later in the week, she asked me to write a *psalm* of my own. It began; *Let me look again into your righteous eyes, my Lord.*

Maybe I'll show it to David. Perhaps he and Eema Lira could set it to music and sing it. Should the next line say, *And open my heart to all you are?*

"Lanee, look at this," Savta would say after music, and off we'd go exploring plants around the lake, Scriptures about the stars, or recipes for sweet-smelling soap. I liked school.

I also liked walking home with Ben. We talked about school, his work, about Beauty, and what he'd seen on the lake that morning. One afternoon he told me that on the night of the feast, he had decided that I was prettier than any girl he'd ever seen. "When, Ben?" I asked. "When you turned around and saw it was I that saved you. I talked so roughly to you because it scared me to feel that way. But later I wanted to be with you, so I came to hide where I saw you hide."

Oh, my! I prayed even harder, *Dear Lord, please save Ben.*

When the Sabbath came, David and Eema Lira arrived for our Friday night meal, and were back the next morning for our prayer meeting. Savta, Yosef, and Abba joined us. After our noon meal, we were all resting in the shadow of the oak in our courtyard.

David broke the silence, "Brother Jonathan, may I ask you a question?"

I ran my hand over the cool honey-colored wood of the table. Abba had built it and the benches for us years ago. *How did he know this wood would feel so cool on a hot day?*

I thought he was napping, leaning so lazily against the tree's trunk, eyes closed, and hands clasped over his middle. Did he hear David's question? After a few moments, he said, "All right." One eyelid cracked. "What is it?"

"Micah let me copy one of the wax tablets Matthew dictated to him." David pulled a small scroll from the bag he carried on his belt. "Look, Brother Jonathan, it says that Jesus told those who believed in Him to be *baptized.*" He unrolled the scroll and squatted down by Abba. "I remember John saying after the Holy Ghost came, some of the disciples were going to baptize the new believers. But after you left, Eema and I continued writing the disciples' testimonies and never went with the others to the pool where they were baptizing. Have you been baptized, Brother Jonathan?"

"No, I haven't. May I look at that scroll more closely?"

Abba was wide-awake now, and took the scroll inside to read its words alone. In just a little while, we heard him praying again. He opened our service the next morning reading from the scroll how Jesus had commanded all believers to be baptized.

"Next Sunday we will meet at Harp's Landing instead of here at the Inn. I want to do what Jesus commanded, and I believe you do, too."

We all agreed. Ben was sitting in the back and heard our plans. After church, I saw David clap him on the shoulder and ask him to come with us Sunday. He didn't reply. I wanted to talk to him, but he left right away for the kitchen. Oh, how I hoped he would come next Sunday! *I'll ask him tomorrow when he walks me home.*

Harp's Landing was a beautiful spot for us to meet. We had gone there many times for picnics. When I asked Abba why it was called by that name, he told me God had made our lake in the shape of a musical harp. The spot called Harp's Landing was at the part of the harp a man would hold it by. I liked that. The shore was scooped in forming a little cove. The grass grew right up to the lake's edge, and plenty of trees shaded the meadow near the shore.

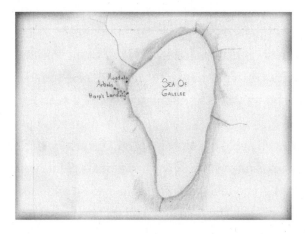

I looked forward to Sunday. After the service, we would have a picnic. Yosef put out a new sign in front of the inn.

BAPTIZING SERVICE–HARP'S LANDING
4TH HOUR SUNDAY–NO SERVICE HERE
ALL ARE WELCOME FOR SERVICE AND MEAL
DINING ROOM CLOSED ALL DAY

Abba studied the scrolls we had, especially the ones that talked about John the Baptist. I looked over his shoulder one night, curious about what he was reading. The olive oil lamp flickered over the words on the scroll.

Abba turned his eyes on me and said, "Do you know why Jesus told us to be baptized, Lanee?"

I answered, "At first I thought it was to wash our sins away, but that can't be, for His blood was shed for that. I really don't know, Abba."

"Pray and ask Jesus to show me how to explain it Sunday, Yonina. I'm not sure about it myself."

That night I asked Jesus for that then I prayed, *and please watch over Ben tonight. I haven't seen him since Sunday, and I don't know why. Help him to be saved soon, Lord. I love him … but you already know that, don't you?*

Thursday afternoon Eema and I had an unexpected visitor. It was Zia! At least Eema recognized her. I could hardly believe she was the same skinny woman I'd seen Jesus heal. She had gained weight and now was quite attractive. Dark curls framed apple cheeks and bright brown eyes. She wore a soft wheat tunic with pale leather sandals. Eema poured her a drink of grape juice and invited her to sit and talk awhile.

"I live over in Magdala now, Cilla. There are about twenty

believers who want to be baptized. Brother Silas was at the Window Inn yesterday and saw the sign about your service. May we come, too?"

Eema turned to me and said, "Lanee, Zia and I have a lot of catching up to do. While we're doing that, will you go to the inn and ask your abba to come home with you? I believe we need to ask him about this."

I left on a run through the trees to the inn. When I got my breath back, I looked for Abba and found him in the stable repairing the gate latch on one of the stalls. When I told him about Zia, he laid his tools aside. We went to the dining room to let Yosef know, and soon were walking briskly back through the trees.

"I think that would be a blessing for us all to have the service together," said Abba after Zia explained her errand. "We were all going to bring food and share a meal. Will that be all right with your people, Sister Zia?"

"Oh, yes. Thank you, Brother Jonathan. I'd better start back so I can tell everyone. We'll meet you at Harp's Landing Sunday morning." She left for Magdala, which was only three miles away on the shore of the lake. Harp's Landing was just south of Magdala.

Watching her hurrying down the road, Abba, with his arms braced against the lintel of the front door, said, "I believe Jesus is planning something special for us this Sunday."

The Sabbath came, and I still hadn't seen Ben since church last week. Why? Was he upset? When he was walking me home those days, nothing had happened but good things. I missed him.

"Abba, has Ben worked all this week?" I asked after our prayer time.

"Yes, he's been coming to work late. Yosef lets him fish in the early morning then go back home to help his abba with his fig harvest. He's been returning in the evening to help serve supper. I would say he's resting today, after such a week."

"Have you been praying for him, Abba?"

"Faithfully, Yonina."

"Me, too."

Sunday morning bright and early we set out the three and a half miles to Harp's Landing. Eema had a basket of food ready, which Abba carried. I took towels, and Eema brought the large blanket to spread our food on. Birds were singing above us in the leafy canopy that shaded the road. It was already hot.

That's one good reason to get into the water today, I told myself. I felt shy about being baptized. It seemed like such a strange thing to do—to wade out in the water and let someone, even if it was Abba, dunk you under. How glad I was that I wouldn't be the only one.

"Abba, did Jesus tell you why He wants us to be baptized?" I asked as we walked.

He nodded and went back to his thoughts. I knew he would tell us all at the service.

When we arrived, Zia and the others from Magdala were already there. The brothers and sisters had thoughtfully set up makeshift tables for the food and had even spread them with colorful cloths. They greeted us with such gladness. Surely, this would be a wonderful day!

Yosef had gone by to pick up Eema Lira, David, and Savta

in the wagon. David hopped out of the wagon bed to carry a big basket of fried fish to the tables. Yosef had brought plates and cups from the inn and a large skin of juice fresh from his ripening vineyard.

It was almost time to begin. Everyone was here. Well, everyone but Ben.

Abba stood out in front us with the lake sparkling behind him. His eyes were serious and thoughtful. He caught my eye and then Eema's. The Lord had given my abba important work to do for Him, and I could see Abba loved it.

He began, "Brothers and sisters, the purpose of our meeting here is to keep Jesus' commandment for believers to be baptized. We know we've been washed from our sins in Jesus' own shed blood. That is not the reason He commands us to be baptized.

Abba walked toward the shore saying, "Brother David and Brother Yosef, will you come with me?" They followed his lead by shucking off their sandals, removing their outer robes, and wading out into the water waist-deep. Abba showed David how to cross his arms over his chest and hold his nose. When they were ready, Abba said, "Jesus said for us to be baptized in the name of the Father and of the Son, and of the Holy Ghost. Brother Yosef and I will take Brother David down in the water. This will show all of you that he has died along with Jesus—that he and all his sins are buried with Christ. When we bring him back up, it is a witness to you that he is now raised with Jesus, a brand new man alive in Christ!"

He looked at David, "Son, is it true?"

David answered joyfully, "Yes, it is, Brother Jonathan!"

"Then I baptize you in the name of the Father, and of the Son, and of the Holy Ghost!" He and Yosef drew David down beneath the water and quickly brought him back up.

David came up and threw his hands in the air. Lake water streamed off his curly black hair, as he shouted toward the sky, "Jesus, I love you, my Lord!"

After seeing David's happy example, why should I fear it?

We formed a line by the shore. As I waited my turn to be taken under, I remembered finding myself in front of Jesus' Cross in Jerusalem. How I had despised it! Now that was all turned around in my mind. Instead of hating His death, I found myself loving His willingness to die for me. It was undeniable proof that He loved me!

I thought, *If I only had the strength to die for you!* Then I knew, *You're not asking me to die right now, are you, Jesus? Maybe you are asking me to die out to my own desires—to be willing to live, but only live to do God's will.*

It was my turn. I stepped out into the cool water and waded to Abba. I had to keep pushing the skirt of my tunic down over my legs until it got good and wet. Thanks to Eema for warning me to wear my thickest one.

The water rose around my body and understanding rose in my mind. *Let the selfish Lanee die, Jesus, and let Lanee, your devoted child, live!* Abba reached his hand out for mine. I crossed my arms and held my nose, and felt Yosef and Abba's hands holding me. "In the name of the Father, and the Son, and the Holy Ghost," Abba declared, and I was swooshed down into the refreshing lake water. Back up I came, feeling new and clean, and completely His. *Oh, thank you, Jesus. You knew I needed this!*

Abba was the last one to have his turn. All the brothers waded out to him and took him under. Abba came up waving his arms crying, "Hallelujah!" The men waded back to shore and the women helped them towel off. Only quiet words were heard. *They must be feeling the awe of it, too.* I went to the shore to hand Abba a towel after I had wrapped mine around my hair. I watched him and Yosef talking together as they waded slowly up out of the water.

A voice, an urgent voice, interrupted the quiet. It came from the direction of the village. At first, I couldn't hear what he was saying. His words grew louder—he must be running. Then I made out the words, "Wait, Brother Jonathan! Wait! Wait, Yosef!" I scanned the trees then caught sight of a figure running through them straight toward us! As he broke out of the trees, he called, "Wait, Brother Jonathan! Wait for me! I can be baptized, now!"

Then I knew. It was Ben!

Oh, what a smile he was wearing! He ran past the shoreline right into the water. He grabbed Abba's hand, then put his arms around him and hugged him.

Yosef exclaimed, "Benjamin ben Jacob, what has happened?"

Ben let go of Abba and hugged Yosef. David and I looked at each other. He put his hand to his heart and pantomimed a bucket dumping over, then waded out in the water to hug Ben, too.

Ben let go of David and turned back to Abba. "Brother Jonathan," he said still breathing hard. "Oh, Brother Jonathan, please don't be angry with me, if I tell you I have fallen in love with your daughter. I cannot explain what has happened to me without telling you that."

He looked at me for the first time. I smiled back, relieved to see him again and so surprised by what he said my face was burning. He held my eyes then turned back toward Abba and said, "The more I loved her, the more impossible it was for me to be with her. Lanee loves Jesus more than she loves anyone, and *I* couldn't love Him. I tried, but I just couldn't.

"And I couldn't come today and just be a spectator. I stayed at home, praying for the help I had to have! All I could think was how can I love someone I really don't know?" He turned to us on the shore and said, "I cried like a baby this morning, wanting to be able to share what you all do with each other—your love for Jesus."

Turning his eyes back to Abba's, he said, "I called on Jesus, then on the Holy Ghost, and finally I remembered the God of our fathers. Somehow, it seemed to me, if it was an impossible situation, He could still get it done.

"I began speaking to Him, reminding myself of His love for us Jews, that we *are* His chosen people. I reached out to Him, searching for His face in my heart."

Ben turned toward us with his eyes blazing. "Suddenly down there on my knees, calling out to our great God—oh how can I tell it? I felt a streak of love shoot out of glory! It penetrated my heart and dug a riverbed down through the center of it. And right now, a channel of love for Jesus is flowing all through me! What I couldn't have, He has given me!"

Suddenly he swung his head around to look at his new friend and said, "David, look, I'm born again!"

Tears fell from his burning black eyes when they found mine and he confessed tenderly, "Oh, Lanee, I am saved."

Ben turned back toward the one standing nearby whose love for Jesus had first made him feel left out, "Yosef, I love Him, too! My Father has helped me! Glory to His name!"

That's when Abba started shouting, then Yosef and David, and all of us on the shore. And Ben stood in the water shouting and speaking in a language he did not know!

Then Abba and Yosef took hold of him, crossed his arms, put his hand on his nose, and took him down under. When he came up shouting, all of us were shouting and speaking in tongues, glorifying our Father, and His Son Jesus, and the precious Holy Ghost for saving us and for saving our Ben!

CHAPTER TWENTY-TWO

OUTCASTS

WHAT a happy feast we had after that! Ben and David's plates were piled high with fried fish, falafel, juicy muskmelon, and fresh bread baked with cheese on top.

Abba thanked the Lord, and we all dug in.

The afternoon turned uncomfortably hot, so after a short rest we packed up and headed home. Eema and Abba walked ahead of us while we carried wet towels and the mostly empty food basket. Ben had taken the blanket out of my hands and was strolling along beside me. My eyes were constantly drawn to his transformed face. Was it God's love shining out of his eyes that made the difference?

He saw my starry-eyed looks and laughed. "Lanee, what are you doing?"

"You're … beautiful." I mumbled.

"I am? Well, you should see *your* face!" He stopped and stared into my eyes, his dancing with joy. "I guess we could just stop awhile and admire each other. But your eema and abba might turn around to see if we've been eaten by a lion." He grabbed my hand and pulled me along. But after a few steps, he stopped suddenly and turned me toward him. His dark lashes gently framed the sweet light in his eyes gazing down into mine.

After a long satisfying moment, I said, "I can't get over how Jesus answered our prayers, Ben. How will I ever repay

Him for what He's done for us?"

"When we were shouting in the water, Lanee, it felt like *that's* what He wanted. He wants us to be blessed by His goodness!" His face glowed with pure joy.

That night on the rooftop, I remembered his joy and cried out with gratitude to the One who gave us such a miraculous day. *Jesus, you saved Ben. Oh, the look on his face when he ran into the water! How I worship you, my Lord! How God must surely love us for He sent you to be our Savior!*

I awoke the next morning dreaming of Ben running through the trees. My first words of the day were, "You did it, Jesus!"

Then I remembered it was our day to take our eggs and cheese to the market. I jumped up and dressed quickly.

Eema and I sell our extras to the grocer on Mondays. Yesterday at the baptizing, I reminded Savta that I would be an hour late for school because of it. She nodded and then asked if we could come by and get hers too. The grocer, Mar Phinehas, was always glad to buy from us, and gave us a fair price for all we brought.

After we picked up Savta's eggs, we had quite a load to carry. Eema and I each lugged a large basket of eggs and a parcel of cheese.

When we reached the market, it was bustling with Monday morning business. Mar Phinehas' grocery shop was all the way down the street right next to the dry goods store. We walked by the apothecary and then by the bakery. My stomach growled at the delightful fresh bread aroma. Maybe Eema would buy us a treat after we finished our business.

"Look, Eema, there's a new seller in the rental booth."

"Those painted pots are lovely. I'll tell Lira about them. Wouldn't that green one fit nicely in her front room?"

I remembered the crowded Jerusalem market, and was glad Arbela's wasn't so busy. Most of the people at our market were neighbors I knew, and almost everyone attended the synagogue.

As we passed the fish market, Eema called out, "Good morning, Sylvia!" Her friend didn't look up from the fish she was examining. *Strange.* We sang out cheery hellos to old Eema Rhoda and her sister Beulah, but they didn't respond. *They must really be losing their hearing.*

"Good morning, Mar Phinehas," Eema said when we stepped into the grocer's fragrant shop. We set our baskets down with relieved sighs. Eema gave him a friendly smile. "Here's more fresh eggs and goat cheese to sell." My mother looked pretty in her pale pink tunic and scarf.

I looked from her to Mar Phinehas, his familiar thick gray-streaked beard blending in with the worn apron tied around his broad middle. He was standing behind an ever-more-cluttered counter. He didn't raise his eyes when he quietly said, "I … uh … I can't use any today." Then he walked around the counter to the pomegranate display at the front of the store.

What? Something is wrong. Mar Phinehas has always greeted us warmly!

Eema and I picked up our baskets and followed him. She spoke up, "Mar Phinehas, don't you remember you told me last week to bring more of everything if we could because sales were up? We've brought our eema's eggs for you today." We smiled and held up our baskets so he could see.

Mar Phinehas stole a look at us then peered behind him, to the right and to the left. He spoke down into the pomegranates in a low voice, "Please, go around to the back door. I will meet you there soon."

We stared at him for a moment and then Eema shrugged and motioned toward the open door. No one looked up at us as we trudged down the street with our full baskets to the alley behind the shops. When I glanced back, I saw our neighbors' faces finally had turned our way.

"What has happened, Eema?"

"I don't know, but I guess we're about to find out."

At the grocer's back door, we set our baskets down and Eema knocked.

Soon Mar Phinehas pulled the door open. He looked both ways down the alley then motioned for us to come in. It was a tiny cramped space jammed with crates of lemons and onions, jugs of olive oil, and burlap sacks of beans and barley.

After we crowded in and set our parcels down, Mar Phinehas said, "Well, um, Priscilla and Lanee, um, I am sorry to tell you I cannot buy from you anymore." His florid face looked sad. "For you see, um, Rabbi ben Tzadik has warned all of us in the synagogue to have, um, no dealings with your family and Yosef. I am terribly sorry for the inn has been my largest account, and you know I have always been glad to get your fresh eggs and cheese."

Eema stared into his troubled eyes. He tore his gaze from hers and said, "Oh, how I wish this Jesus of Nazareth had never come here!"

We glanced at each other, disturbed by his words. Then Eema said, "Mar Phinehas, may I speak to you for just a few moments?"

He nodded reluctantly, being a naturally polite man. "For only a *few* moments—I need to get back up front to see to my customers."

"I'll not take long." She tipped her head back to look into his solemn eyes. "Mar Phinehas, can you remember the first time I sold you my extra eggs?"

"Yes, Priscilla, it was before Lanee was born."

"Do you recall what I told you that day?"

Looking out from under his bushy eyebrows into Eema's eyes, he sighed and said, "Though it was long ago, yes, I still remember it." He looked away from her and picked up a bag of barley. He piled it on top of some other bags and untied the top. As he ran his fingers through the grain, he said, "You were terribly sad. I remember you cried and said, 'I am so lonely. My husband must work long hours at the inn and then more, building our house, and I am always busy preparing for the baby and for the house.

"'Though I am busy,' you said, 'I am growing lonelier every day.'" Mar Phinehas absent-mindedly sifted barley, picking out bits of straw. "Then I remember you suddenly looked ashamed. I thought you realized you were talking too personally to me, a stranger."

Eema sought Mar Phinehas' eyes. "Do you also recall what you told me that day?"

"Yes, um, Priscilla, I do." He dug his hands deeper into the bag of grain. "I said, 'Please don't think of it. It is the way of life—that loneliness. Everyone feels it, but we all learn to live around it.' I gave you my handkerchief to dry your eyes. Then I bought your eggs and cheese."

"Mar Phinehas, when you said it, I knew you were telling me the truth. I did dry my eyes and made up my mind not to cry over my loneliness anymore. When Lanee was born and the house was built, I didn't feel it as much. But, as you said, it was always there. Sometimes in the same room with Lanee and Jonathan, I still felt lonely. But, Mar Phinehas, the day that Jesus came, my loneliness left!"

Suddenly he pulled his hands out of the bag and briskly brushed them off on his apron. "Oh, no, Priscilla, don't speak of it to me." He looked her square in the face. "Do you want me to be cast out of the synagogue?"

He re-tied the barley bag then said, "I will buy your eggs and cheese today, but don't bring them again. My business would not survive if I were not a part of the synagogue."

He reached out his burly arms and took our cheese parcels, then started emptying the baskets of eggs into the nearby crates. All the time he counted the eggs, his expression grew more and more perplexed. When he finished, he pulled some coins from his apron pocket and handed them to us.

It wasn't until he opened the door for us to leave that

he looked at Eema again. His sad brown eyes couldn't help saying what his whisking us out did not say—*I will miss you.*

We hurried from the marketplace as if we were being chased.

"Eema what will happen to us here?" I asked as we turned down the road to the inn. *Lord, I'm afraid.*

"It is in Jesus' hands, daughter. They crucified Him; perhaps we will suffer such, too."

When Eema said His name, calmness settled over me. *Be not afraid, it is I!* Matthew's scroll had said.

At the inn, Abba met us with a smile and a kiss. He was surprised to see Eema with me. When she told him about Mar Phinehas, he called a meeting of the church, all except David who was at ben Judah's farm. This time, my Ben was also included.

After we told them of the rabbi's decree, Yosef said, "Well, that explains it! Saul, my produce supplier, didn't show up this morning. Also, several who have eaten their morning meal here for years did not come."

Then Ben said, "I hadn't told you yet, Yosef, but this morning Abba asked me to quit my job here. When he did, I told him about the Lord saving me and about the baptizing. He didn't know what to say. I thought I saw tears in his eyes. He let me come on to work today." Ben's eyes met mine. His look of joy had dimmed.

"We need to pray," Abba said.

So we all knelt to ask the Lord's help. I couldn't help crying as I prayed. I was so happy that Ben had come to Jesus and thrilled that he loved me, but right on top of that glad experience came this sad encounter with Mar Phinehas.

Jesus, please don't let us lose the joy that you gave us. And, oh, Jesus, will you save Mar Phinehas?

After our prayer, Yosef told Eema, "From now on I will buy your eggs and cheese, Cilla. Also, Jonathan, we must find a produce dealer in Magdala or if necessary as far away as Tiberius. The inn will survive without the local trade, though I will miss seeing our neighbors."

Everyone went back to work, Eema went home, and Savta and I finally started our school day. She gave me a big smile and said our first lesson would come from the Book of Esther in the Scriptures.

"Lanee, I want you to understand our people have always dealt with the threat of persecution. It is strange for it to be coming to us from our own Jewish neighbors. Nevertheless, I would like you to see that God offers great opportunities along with persecution. Will you look for that as you study Esther, and as you continue to live in Arbela?"

I got busy reading Esther from Yosef's old scroll. It told of a beautiful Jewish girl, Esther, who in captivity was chosen to be King Ahasuerus' queen. When one man, Haman, plotted to destroy the Jews, Esther's cousin, Mordecai, urged her to go to the king for help. Esther courageously came before the king, risking the death penalty, in order to beg him to spare her people. He granted her request by hanging Haman and allowing the Jews to fight for themselves. Because of Esther's bravery, the Jews were lifted up to a place of great respect in the kingdom.

When I finished, I saw Savta standing at the window looking toward Arbela. She didn't appear to be troubled about the rabbi and the village turning against us.

She looked around at me and said, "Now we have studied about two Jewish queens, Queen Alexandria and Queen Esther. They were both great Jewish women whom God used to help our people. Perhaps God will use you, my granddaughter, or me, an old woman, to help our people to believe in His Son, here in Arbela."

I remembered how cousin Mordecai told Esther, "Perhaps you have come to the kingdom for such a time as this." And as Savta stood gazing out toward our village with love and hope, I began to hope, too.

Chapter Twenty-Three

Deborah Visits

"Lanee! Come out here and see what I've got!"

David's musical voice reached me in my room.

"I'll be right down, David," I called back.

When I stepped out our front door, he was standing there holding a rope tied to a brown and white cow.

"Her name is Tiny," he explained.

"Where'd you get her?"

"I traded some work at ben Judah's for her."

He dropped down in the shade of the sycamore tree. Tiny immediately began munching on the grass growing under the tree.

David looked up at me with a mysterious smile. "Guess who I met today?"

"Tell me!" I said as I sat down beside him.

The gorgeous smile grew wider when he said, "Your friend, Deborah."

"Oh, really? Isn't she pretty, David?" From the sparkle in his stormy eyes, I knew he agreed. "How did you meet her?"

"Her abba took me to his dairy barn to introduce me to Tiny, she came looking for him, and we met. You should have seen her abba's face when she started petting Tiny. Surprised isn't the word for it. He even said, 'Deborah, I've never seen you interested in my cows before. Are you feeling all right?'"

"It was you, David, wasn't it? It was *you*!"

He gave me a big grin. "She knew I knew, and her face

turned even prettier when she blushed."

"I've never seen her blush!"

Suddenly I remembered David didn't know what had happened to us at Mar Phinehas' store. "Oh, David, I need to tell you some news."

He saw my troubled expression and said, "What is it?"

His face grew sober as I told him all about our encounter with Mar Phinehas, about Yosef's loss of customers and vendors, and about Ben's abba wanting him to quit his job. Then I told him about Savta's lesson.

"When I read the Book of Esther, David, I saw that many times persecution comes from one person in power. In Esther, it was Haman. But God helped Esther defeat Haman's desires to destroy God's people. Rabbi ben Tzadik has commanded the members of the synagogue to have no dealings with us. We must pray God defeats his counsel."

David replied, "Yes, but at the same time, we must obey what Jesus said in Matthew's scroll. He said to 'resist not evil' and to 'love our enemies.' We must remember to treat Rabbi ben Tzadik as Jesus would have us to."

"I haven't thought of that, David. I will try to obey Him. And I know the Holy Ghost will help me."

Lord, I appreciate my friend, I thought as I watched David head for home with Tiny clumping along behind. Would ben Judah fire him? At least he hadn't today.

Later in the week, David showed up at the inn just as I got out of school. He was in the kitchen talking to his eema when I looked in.

"Well, Lanee, the sword fell today. Ben Judah stopped me in the field and asked if I was a believer. I said, 'Yes, Jesus

Christ is my Savior.' He put his big hand on my shoulder, father-like, and said, 'Son, I like your work, and it's been enjoyable having you here, but I can't employ you anymore, Here's your pay, and a little extra to help you as you find another job.' Then he walked away."

"Oh, no, David."

"That's not all. My two work mates were standing by and heard what he said. They went after him and said, 'Ben Judah, we also believe in Jesus. You'd better fire us too.' That hit him pretty hard. They've been with him for years and are two of his best workers. He told them to follow him to the house so he could get their pay."

David continued, his eyes wide with wonder, "Then I noticed them following me on the road home. I called, 'Simon, James, when did you start believing in Jesus?'

"They caught up to me, and Simon said, 'The moment you said He was your Savior, that was the moment I began to believe in Him. If He can have a man like you, He can have me!'

"Then James said, 'Your heart was in your face, boy, and it told me the truth. Can we have Him like you do, David?'

"I said, 'Jesus said to believe in Him and repent of your sins.' We went aside into the trees and knelt down. Both of them repented with tears. This Sunday, we'll have two new members in our church!"

The kitchen got loud then! We shouted our praise to the One who had turned bad into good. When Yosef and Abba heard, they sent for Simon and James to go to work for Yosef's partner in the fields. Yosef asked David to work at the inn—he had lost more help since the rabbi's decree.

After all the excitement, Ben took a break to walk me home. He took my hand and led me to the path through the trees.

"Do I owe you an apology, Lanee?" It was the first time we had been alone since the baptizing. I glanced over at him. How appealing he was in his brown linen tunic and wide leather belt. His black hair shone in the afternoon sunlight.

"I don't know. For what, Ben?"

"I've been thinking that I should have told you first that I loved you—before I told your abba and eema and the whole church."

"Ben ..." I sought his eyes.

"Yes?" He looked back at me from under his thatch of hair.

"We told each other when I was twelve and you were fifteen."

He stopped and turned me toward him. "I didn't understand it then. You were so little! And I didn't even want a girlfriend. I decided just to ignore you. But it turned out, I couldn't." His eyes grew wide with amazement. "How wonderful are the Lord's ways! He wanted us to love each other so I could be saved!"

After a long moment, he said, "When this trouble with my abba is resolved, may I ask him to visit your abba about us?"

Into the wonderful dark eyes of the boy at the well, now a young man, I answered, "Yes, I would like that very much, Ben."

He bent his head and brushed my lips with his. Holding hands, we walked on home. I was up the stairs in my room before I heard a "Whoop, wooie!" from the direction of the woods.

I laughed.

Jesus, we'll love you. Jesus, we'll serve you. Oh, thank you, Savior, for my dear Ben.

Now Ben and I had our secret. Though he'd told everyone he loved me, no one knew we were promised to each other. I didn't want anyone else to know. Not yet. My birthday would soon be here, and I would be fifteen. I wanted to guard my secret at least until then.

At school the next day, Savta said, "Lanee, you're just glowing today. You must have had a really good night's sleep." I just smiled and kept working on my computations. Soon the school day would end and hopefully Ben would walk beside me forever—I mean ... home. *Such daydreaming!*

He was standing near the door when I stepped out, only to tell me he was working in the kitchen and couldn't take a break. He looked around and kissed me lightly again. *I love you, Ben,* I thought. Aloud I said, "I'll see you tomorrow."

"Eema! I'm home!" I called out as I entered the front door.

"Out back, Lanee!"

I went on through the cool house to the courtyard. There sitting with my mother, enjoying a cup of Eema's sweet pomegranate juice, was Deborah.

She looked up at me and said, "I wasn't sure when you got home from school." Dressed in her lovely pink tunic with a soft flowered scarf covering her curls, she was quite a contrast to Eema in her working clothes.

"We've been sharing stories about our favorite teacher— your savta," Eema informed me. "Well Deborah, you are in good hands now. I'll get back to my garden." She got up and gave me a kiss on the cheek then left for the back courtyard.

"I'm surprised." I poured myself a cup of the juice and offered her some more.

"I have enough, thank you." Her pretty eyes looked into mine then fell to the cup she was holding between delicately laced fingers. "Lanee, may I talk to you about something? Uh, I mean, some*one*?

"Who is it?"

"I believe his name is David." She blushed! And she *did* look prettier.

I couldn't help smiling, remembering David's description of her petting Tiny.

"The most handsome boy I've ever met," I said.

"Oh, yes, Lanee. Where is he from? How long have you known him? How old is he? What is his family like? Where does he live?"

"Wait Deborah. First of all, you need to know that he is a believer in Jesus Christ. He, too, is filled with the Holy Ghost. And also you need to know your abba fired him yesterday."

She looked startled—I'm not sure about which of the statements I'd made. "That can't be true. Abba told me he is an excellent worker. He has caught on quickly to every task he has given him. And he's conscientious about working the amount of time he's paid for. My abba gave him one of our best dairy cows in trade for wages. He never does that for anyone!"

"Deborah, your visit here tells me that either you don't know or you've forgotten the rabbi has forbidden all of you to have any dealings with us believers."

"What?"

"We found it out Monday, and yesterday your abba fired

David for following Jesus."

"We didn't go to the synagogue on the Sabbath. We went to Jerusalem and weren't back until Monday."

"So the rabbi must have visited your abba then with his warning."

Deborah's brow knitted. "First, I can't go to your savta's school, and now David is fired! Why?"

"Why was Jesus crucified?" I asked, staring into her frustrated eyes.

She looked away. In a moment, she turned back and asked, "Lanee, will you help me to get to know David? When I first saw him, I knew I'd met the one man I could love. Please don't laugh. I can't get him out of my mind. When I heard you were his friend, I just had to come to you and learn more about ..."

"Lanee! Can you come out? I brought you something!"

The melodic voice that was calling me from our front yard was David's.

CHAPTER TWENTY-FOUR

DEBORAH MEETS JESUS

I F David could have only seen us then, how he would have laughed. Could I compare us to two of those musht suddenly dropped on the bottom of Yosef's boat? Our eyes just bugged out!

Then I smiled and asked her, "Do you want to see him?"

"Yes. May I?"

Who was this girl speaking to me in such a meek voice? We left the courtyard for the front door.

"What did you bring me, David?" I spoke as I walked the last few steps. "Not a cow, I hope!"

He was wearing his best white-toothed smile when I reached the doorway, and when he saw Deborah behind me, his eyes really lit up.

"Please excuse me, Lanee; I didn't know you had company." He looked past me and greeted her, "Hello, Deborah."

I turned and saw her give him the sweetest, most sincere smile, the likes of which I had never seen on Deborah's face. "I'm glad to see you again, David." *Is this a dream?*

I looked back at David and noticed he was holding one of his arms behind his back. Whatever he had brought me, must be behind there. I didn't have long to wait, for he pulled his arm out and said, "Well, Lanee, here she is!"

It was the tiniest kitten I'd ever seen. Her fur was a neat pattern of black, yellow, and white, making her look all dressed up! Each of her feet had white socks on. I reached for the little cat. Next to a donkey, how I'd wanted my own kitten! "Oh, she is so pretty! Where did you get her?"

"Yosef's partner was giving them away this morning. The mother had disappeared—probably killed by a wild animal. I hope I wasn't wrong in believing you might like this little one."

"Wait here, David. I'll ask Eema!"

I'll call her Susanna! She'll sleep in my room! I carried her cradled in my arms out to where Eema was gathering onions. "Eema, look what David brought!" I said, holding Susanna out. She brushed her hands off and took her.

"How sweet. She is very young. Where is her mother?"

"David said the kittens were left alone. He thinks her mother was killed. May I keep her, Eema?"

Eema petted her a little, and then carefully handed her back to me, "Yes, she can stay. Maybe she'll grow up to be a good mouser. We could use one."

I walked back through the house and heard David telling Deborah he was working at the inn again.

"I'm sorry my abba fired you, David. He found no fault

in your work."

David smiled down at her and said, "It's perfectly all right. If I'd still been there, Lanee wouldn't have her kitten." When he saw me, he sang out, "She's letting you keep her! Hallelujah! What will you name her?"

"Her name is Susanna. And look, she's fallen asleep in my arms." *She trusts me! Oh, I have a kitten!* "I already love her, David!"

He nodded and said, "I need to get back to the inn to help serve supper." Looking at Deborah, he said, "Lanee, bring Deborah to church Sunday, all right?"

"I'll try. Thank you for my little Susanna, David."

When he was gone, Deborah and I took the sleeping kitten to my room. We sat on my mat together. As I stroked Susanna's furry little head, I said, "You know, you haven't officially been told not to associate with us. Would you like to visit our church on Sunday?"

"May I?"

Lord, who is this girl sitting beside me on this mat?

After she left, I thought, *Could it be possible that Deborah would come to our church?* Then I realized she'd already done the impossible when she visited my house.

At our prayer meeting when the Sabbath came, I squeezed my pillow down by the stairs, earnestly asking Jesus to save Deborah.

Sunday morning we gathered in the Window Room all excited with the increase in our congregation. Zia and some of the believers from Magdala had come. They filled up the second row of seats. James with his wife, and Simon, with his wife and children filled up the third row. Ben and I,

David, and the rest of our church all sat in front. It was just about time to start when someone else arrived. A mighty mountain of a man stepped in and behind him petite and beautiful Deborah.

The big man, whom I remembered as her bodyguard, sat in the very last row, and Deborah took a seat behind James and Simon. They turned around and greeted her. I glanced at David, and together we went to her.

"You came!" we said at the same time. Then David said, "Would you like us to sit with you?"

She said, "Yes, please." He sat down, and I went back up to Ben and asked him to join us. We took the inside seats next to them.

"I hope you don't mind that Zibeon came with me. Abba allows me much freedom to go where I like, if he goes too."

"Does your abba know you are here today?" I asked.

"No," she said.

Abba started the service. "Would anyone like to testify of the Lord's goodness to you this past week?"

James stood right up. "He saved me, Brother Jonathan!" A big smile lit his sunburned face.

When he sat down, Simon, who was strong and friendly and had an upturned nose, stood and said, "Jesus saved me, too. And last night he saved my wife and all my children!" He swept his arm out toward them, and the whole family stood up and smiled at us. The children all looked like little Simons with the same nose in miniature.

Abba said with joy, "Looks like we're going to need another baptizing service." We all began to thank and praise the Lord. The three of us stood and raised our hands, rejoicing that James and Simon belonged to Jesus now. Deborah remained seated.

Abba asked David and Eema Lira to sing. They went up to the podium and sang,

> "What happened when I picked
> The sweet Rose of Sharon?
> The fairest of ten thousand
> Chose me for His own;
> What happened when my Lord Jesus
> Called me to Him?
> He, so meek and lowly,
> Never leaves me alone."

I had never heard a song sung like that one. David sang his strong bass melody, and his mother sang an airy tune above him. The two melted together into what must have been harmony fit for Heaven. Their song spoke of loneliness quenched, of longings satisfied. I thought of the life they lived before Jesus came. *How great a Savior you are, Lord Jesus!*

I peeked at Deborah while they sang. Her eyes were closed, and a soft smile curved her lips.

They finished and David returned to his seat. I heard Deborah whisper to him, "Lovely." He gave her a gentle smile.

Abba said, "I have asked Sister Zia to give her testimony for our sermon today. Will you come now, Sister?"

Zia, looking pretty with dark bushy curls framing her face, walked up to the pulpit. She gave us a smile and said, "I met Jesus on the Galilean hills right out from your village. Some of you were there the day I met Him. I was a hopeless shell of a woman. I was a freak to my family. My own eema couldn't stand to look at me. I lay on my mat day after day in horrible pain, believing my suffering would never end. The day my dod carried me from Magdala to your hillside, I had been trying to figure out how I could end my life."

She paused and gazed at us young people with her big brown eyes. Sister Zia glowed with good health. I might not have believed she was telling the truth, if I hadn't seen her the day she was healed.

"When I was your age, Lanee, I was perfectly normal," she said. "In fact, I was never sick. Priscilla's family knew my family. Often we ran together, played chase, and other games. One day when I was seventeen, I had a hot fever. After that, I became crippled. Then my body grew more and more deformed with every passing day."

Sister Zia came around the pulpit and walked to the back row, where Zibeon sat with his arms folded over his chest. We turned around following her movements.

"Mar Zibeon, do you remember me?"

His voice rumbled out of his chest, "Yes, I surely do. I helped carry you from your dod's wagon to the place where Jesus was."

"Did you see Jesus heal me?"

"Yes, I did."

"Do you believe in Him, Mar Zibeon?"

"Does He want me to, Sister Zia? I am just a slave."

"Yes, He does."

"Yes? Yes! I do believe in you, Jesus!" Then the giant man jumped up and cried out, "If you'll have me, Lord, I'll be yours from now on!" He raised his hands and began to wave them and shout.

Deborah had turned around to watch with the rest of us.

Suddenly she stood up and sailed out the door. Before I could even think, I was on my feet running after her.

I found her on the stone bench under the lowering branches of the mulberry tree. She was crying. When I put my arm around her shoulders, she protested in between sobs, "I didn't come ... to get to ... know Jesus. I came to be ... with David." Then she cried even harder, "Oh, Lanee, He's calling me to Him. What shall I do?"

I hugged her to me and said, "You need Jesus, Deborah. He knows you do."

"Lanee! Just now, I almost told you to take your arms off me. It was in my mind to run home to Abba and tell on Zibeon—to run away from Jesus. But Lanee—don't let go of me! I'm tired of being an unloving, cold, sulky child. You are so right!" Suddenly she wasn't talking to me anymore. "How I need you, Jesus! Please, give me your love. Please, let me love you." Then she cried even harder.

I looked up when I heard a step beside us. It was Mar Zibeon.

"There, there, Little Sister, Jesus has heard you. Don't cry anymore, Little Sister. He is healing your poor soul, like He just did mine."

I looked up into a broad black face, covered in tears. The tenderness on that face, the like I had never seen before.

Deborah's crying subsided. She turned to me and hugged me fully. She was sweet with the fragrance of some expensive ointment—the way a fresh white lily would smell. It was the first time we'd ever hugged.

In her tight hug, I heard her say, "I believe in Jesus, Lanee." She spoke again over my shoulder to her faithful slave, her voice still filled with tears, "Oh, Zibeon, He *has* heard me and saved me."

After a few moments of quiet, she pulled back to look into my eyes, and asked, "*Now* what are we going to do?"

Deborah didn't know it, but the same question had troubled us all for the past week. I noticed the church was standing around, having followed us out into the courtyard. David and Ben were nearby. David's tears were shining on his face. I saw that both he and Ben were still praying silently.

Hearing Deborah's question, Eema and Savta both came close to comfort her. Eema knelt in front of her and answered her question, "Sister Deborah, we're going to love Jesus and each other, and we're going to pray."

Savta had placed her firm hand on her slim shoulder. Deborah reached up and covered it with hers then began to cry again. "Already He has begun to bless me. Oh, my teacher, I have missed you so!"

It was a long time before we were ready to leave the sweet-smelling Yafe Perach where Deborah had met Jesus. Brother Zibeon finally said, "Little Sister, we'd better go now."

As they walked to their carriage, I remembered how I had always longed to be Deborah's close friend. Tears began to flow over my cheeks as I watched them go. *Thank you, my Sweet Rose of Sharon, for giving me another desire of my heart!*

CHAPTER TWENTY-FIVE

IF MY PEOPLE WILL PRAY

TWO exciting things were happening Sunday: All our new brothers and sisters were going to be baptized at Harp's Landing, and afterward, we'd all celebrate my birthday with a picnic! I could hardly wait.

I was teaching Susanna to lap milk from a dish. My little kitty sometimes suckled against my side probing me with her paws as if I were her mother. It touched my heart for her—poor little orphan.

Every day I prayed for Deborah. I hadn't seen or heard from her since Sunday. What had happened when she and Mar Zibeon had gone home?

Things seemed to settle down as our church and the synagogue went our separate ways. At least that's how it *seemed*. We still went to the well for our water, but we bought our supplies from Yosef. We wanted to live at peace with the rest of the village as best we could.

Somehow, I had to get word to Deborah about the baptizing Sunday. But, how? Every day I looked in vain for her at the well. I went to the playground, hoping she'd be there. I found she wasn't, but Sarah was. The rabbi's daughter was sitting under our oak with Misha and Elisabeth.

"Lanee!" she called out, "we are not allowed to converse with you, so please don't even try."

Elisabeth looked sad, and it sounded as if Sarah wasn't too proud of herself right then. I just nodded my head and turned back toward home, feeling discouraged. A way down the dusty road I saw a carriage stopped beside the road. Drawing nearer to it I saw the man who held the reins was a huge black man—Brother Zibeon! He was waiting for me.

"Sister Lanee," he called as I approached, "I have a message for you from Little Sister." I came up to the side of the carriage and looked up into his large brown eyes. "She said her abba will not let her come back to the church, and she asked you to pray for her. She wanted to know how Susanna and David are."

"What happened, Brother Zibeon?"

"My master met us at the door, asking where we had been. He knew Little Sister was interested in David. We told him the truth—all of it. That's when Mar ben Judah forbade her to return, and he also forbade me. He couldn't fire me—one doesn't fire one's slave." He chuckled when he said that.

The news wasn't good, but at least it was news. "Please tell Deborah, I'm praying for her every day. Susanna is learning to eat from a dish and sleeps right beside me. David asks every day if I've seen her. And tell her we are going to Harp's Landing on Sunday to baptize all the new brothers and sisters, and to celebrate my birthday. I'm praying for Jesus to open the way for you and Deborah to come. Please tell her Jesus will never leave her, and that she must hold on to Him."

"Thank you, child. I'll be going on now. Ask your abba to pray for me. Tell him I've never been so happy in all my life, except for not being allowed to come back to church." He gave me a hearty smile before he turned the carriage toward the ben Judah farm.

That evening David and Eema Lira came for supper and brought a surprise—Ben came with them! When Savta showed up too, I knew something was happening. Abba told me what, as we fed the chickens and gathered the eggs. "We need to pray together tonight, Lanee. The Lord has shown me if we will pray then He will save our neighbors and friends. After supper Yosef, James, and Simon will be here too.

"Abba," I said, "Brother Zibeon and Deborah are forbidden to come back to the church. We must pray about that too."

"Oh, no. But, I thought that would happen. Tell everyone about them before we pray, Yonina, for only the Lord can work this out."

When I carried in my basket of eggs, I saw Ben was helping Eema prepare our meal. He looked up from the salad greens he was tearing and winked at me. He had never even been inside our house before, and here he was cooking beside my eema! I washed my hands and poured juice in cups, which David helped me carry to our dining mat.

"Did you hear from Deborah today?" he asked. We were alone arranging the cups and dishes around the mat.

"Yes, I did. Her abba knows all about last Sunday and won't let her come back to church. Brother Zibeon brought her message to me. She asked about Susanna and you."

"I wonder if it would help if I talked to Mar ben Judah."

"David! Don't you remember he fired you?"

"He also laid his hand on my shoulder and called me 'son.'"

"Do you think he was prophesying?" I said in a teasing voice.

"Lanee, would you like me to tell you what I really think?"

I sure would, I thought, though I didn't get a chance to

say it, for right then everyone came to sit down for supper. The fish chowder, salad with olive oil and vinegar, and fresh buttered barley bread looked delicious. I sat by Ben and held his hand when Abba thanked the Lord for the food.

While the others were chatting, he leaned over and whispered in my ear, "How pretty you are tonight, Lanee!" I turned and smiled into his dark eyes. Then he said, "One day I'll not just visit here, but I'll be a son in your home."

"You will be dearly loved, Ben," I whispered back. It was the closest I'd ever come to telling him aloud, *I love you.*

After supper, we helped with the dishes. Then Yosef came with Brother James and Brother Simon, and we all gathered on the rooftop. Abba asked the church to pray for our friends and neighbors to be saved, for the Lord had assured him that if we would pray, they would be.

Next I told them what Brother Zibeon had told me and asked, "Please pray that he and Sister Deborah and will be able to be baptized Sunday."

"Oh, how Rabbi ben Tzadik needs his eyes opened to believe in Jesus," Eema said, "Please, pray for him, too."

With such a load of serious needs, we all found a private spot on the rooftop to kneel down, and began pouring our hearts out to the Savior. I felt so weighed down, I could hardly speak. Then I remembered how the Holy Ghost had always helped me since Pentecost, and I began to hope for His help with the heavy load. As soon as the desire came, He fell on me, speaking through me in an unknown tongue. I let Him speak, and speak, and speak, knowing the One who knew about it all was praying for every need.

I began to hear the others moved on by the Holy Ghost.

It wasn't loud and strong as many times before, rather it sounded sad and sweet. We yielded, and He prayed. Soon I heard Brother James' and Brother Simon's voices along with ours, allowing the Holy Ghost to pray through them. I don't know how long we prayed, but when the Holy Ghost lifted, we knew it was enough.

Everyone was leaving for home. Abba started out walking with Savta. David and Eema Lira were loading up in the wagon with Yosef and the others. After he helped his eema up onto the seat, he leaned over to me and said, "I'll tell you tomorrow," with a mysterious smile. I nodded, feeling very curious about my friend's secret.

Ben said, "Shalom," to Eema then I walked with him as far as the sycamore tree at our front door. We were alone for the first time. He lifted my chin so I was gazing into his eyes. "I'm so astounded by all of this! Do you remember when I asked you what you thought of Jesus? Did you know then that He could bring us into such experiences with God?"

"Not really. But I did find out the first day I met Him, He knows God better than anyone ever has. And Ben, Jesus shared God immediately with me that first day."

He pulled me to him and hugged me. "And now I'm in love with both of you, Lanee! It's amazing!"

Yes, Jesus, you are amazing!

CHAPTER TWENTY-SIX

IT'S MY BIRTHDAY!

WHEN I opened my eyes, the first thing that popped into my head was *I'm fifteen!* I grabbed my sheet and headed out to the rooftop.

The early morning air was cool and inviting. I watched a pair of cranes fly over. The hills back of our courtyard were brown, not spring green as they were when we'd met Jesus. As soon as I thought of Him, I wanted to pray. *Thank you, Jesus, for my family and Ben. Thank you for saving me, and for the Holy Ghost living in me. Oh, Savior, will you let Deborah and Brother Zibeon come and be baptized today, if it be your will? Thank you that I'm fifteen today, Lord, and that you're with me.*

I marveled as I thought about Deborah—how different she was. Her meeting David had started it all, but then, wonder of wonders, she'd asked Jesus into her heart.

It amazed me when I found a note on my desk the next morning after our prayer meeting. I unfolded the sheet of expensive parchment and read, "We're coming! Love, Sister Deborah"

"How?" I'd spoken aloud.

Savta heard my exclamation and said, "What is it, Lanee?" When I showed her Deborah's note, she smiled and nodded, remembering one little girl's determined ways. Even so, we fervently asked Jesus in our morning prayer to help her and Brother Zibeon.

After school that afternoon, it wasn't Ben who came to walk me home, but David. "Ben asked me to tell you he's out in the vineyard today, Lanee. So, may I have the pleasure of escorting you home?"

I smiled up at him, thinking he'd like to hear the great news of Deborah's note. "Yes, David, especially since you promised to tell me all about being Daniel ben Judah's son-in law."

David led me out the courtyard to the dirt road home. I took a deep breath of the fresh air, trying to be patient to hear what he had to say and to tell him my news. The summer was losing its hold on the country. I imagined Ben at work turning rows of shriveled grapes over, so they'd dry in the sun into perfect raisins. What *was* David going to say? When I let myself peer back at him, he was really grinning.

"Curious, aren't you, Lanee?" he said.

"David, dearest friend of mine, will you please just tell me?"

"All right, I will. First, though, will you promise until I release you from it, you won't tell anyone what I say?"

"I promise, Lord willing."

"What?"

"Only if the Lord told me otherwise will I ever tell it, David."

"That'll do."

He stopped (so I did, too), took a deep breath, looked into my eyes as serious as I've ever seen him, and said, "The Lord wants me to marry Deborah."

"David!" I was shocked. "How do you know?"

His expression grew tender and he looked more

comely than ever before. He said, "I felt it in my heart when I saw her delicate hand pet Tiny's head that first day we met."

Then I couldn't help it. I laughed. And laughed. And laughed.

"Lanee! Lanee! Don't do this to me. Why are you laughing?"

"I'm sorry, David. You laughed, too. Remember?"

"Yes, but now it doesn't seem so funny that such a girl would try to come down to earth to be with me. I'm smitten, Lanee."

"And you believe the Lord has smitten you with her?"

"Yes, especially after what happened Sunday."

We started walking again.

"So that's what I think," he said, "What do you think?"

I looked at my sandals not knowing what to tell him, when suddenly I felt the Holy Ghost move in my heart. Wide-eyed with wonder, I answered his question, "I believe the Lord's hand is upon both of you."

He saw my look then gazed off down the road, nodding his curly head. "It's true, just as I thought. But, pray for us, Lanee. I'm half Jew, half Roman, and all Christ's, which her abba fired me for. I'm poor and she is rich. How could that work? Only the Lord can bring about His will for us."

"I will pray, David." I smiled up into my best friend's troubled eyes. "Oh, I have something to tell you, too! Deborah sent me a note today! Somehow, she managed to get it on my desk at school. It said, 'We're coming! Love, Sister Deborah.'"

David slapped his leg and exclaimed, "I knew it!"

"But *how* will she be able to come, David?"

"Lanee, how did the Holy Ghost fill us? There is nothing too hard for God!"

"There is nothing too hard for God." I thought as I breathed in the morning air of my fifteenth birthday. *All right, Jesus, I believe Deborah and Brother Zibeon will be baptized today.*

Back in my room, I put on the new clothes we'd made for the feast. This was my first occasion since then to dress up in the linen tunic and embroidered scarf. It's my birthday, besides being the day when many new believers will be baptized.

Cuddling Susanna in my arms, I came down the stairs. Eema turned from gazing out toward the court, opened her arms and said, "Who is this young lady descending our stairs so regally? Could it be my baby, who only yesterday took her first step?"

I put Susanna down and went to her for my birthday hug. Abba came in from the courtyard and got his. "We've made you a present, Yonina. It's out back," he said.

What could it be?

I followed them outside and discovered a large open cedar chest waiting under the oak. Inside the fragrant box lay a folded spread woven from the skein of blue yarn Eema had bought at the market stall in Jerusalem.

"Oh, Eema, you made me this?" I gathered its soft lushness up to my face. It smelled of cedar and Eema.

"Dod Ethan brought me more of the yarn when he came last month." She smiled proudly into my delighted eyes. Gently she took it from my hands, folded it, and placed it back in the chest. Then Abba closed the lid.

Oh, look what Abba has done! I knelt so I could run my fingers over the lovely gift. The chest was silky smooth all over, except in the center of the lid, where a figure had been skillfully carved. It was a dove resting in a man's hand.

Abba and Eema stood on the other side of the chest watching my face. "How beautiful it is. Oh, Abba, is that your hand holding me?"

"No, my daughter. That is how it *was*. This hand belongs to 'the son of the right hand,' who is Benjamin."

"Oh, my! Abba and Eema, do you know?"

"Yes, Yonina, we know," said Abba. "When Ben was saved, we knew *God's* hand was moving to bring your marriage to pass."

Then Eema said, "We will welcome Benjamin to our family, Lanee."

I knew my face was red, but I felt so glad they knew, I didn't care. Eema ran her hand over the chest and said, "During the year of your betrothal we will fill up your new chest with lovely things for your wedding and home."

I arose from my knees and went to her. Holding me in

her arms, she said, "I love you, Lanee."

It felt confusing—I was excited to be fifteen—but I still wanted to be my eema's little girl! My abba, who always understood me, put his arms around both of us and said, "Don't worry, Yonina. You'll always be our baby."

After we carried my chest with its lovely contents upstairs, I took a moment to enjoy my gift alone. My room seemed different to me now. Little Susanna had found her way back upstairs and was napping on my mat. I ran my fingers over the dove in Ben's hand. I thought, *My life is changing—yet it's a good change. It's becoming more and more complete.*

Then I hurried downstairs. Today was my birthday!

Our arms were loaded down with the food and towels as we left for Harp's Landing. We stepped out of the tree-lined road to the lakeshore and found Zia and the Magdala church busy setting up tables for the food.

Ben was helping set up the last one. When he saw me, a beautiful smile broke over his face. I returned his smile with all the happiness the morning had brought me and went to him, slipping my hand into his.

"I was hoping you'd get here a little early," he said squeezing my hand. "Come with me quickly, before the service starts!"

"What is it, Ben?" He didn't answer but steered me over to the large willow tree near the shore. He parted the wispy branches and picked up his towel. Under it, he'd hidden a package wrapped in a blue cloth.

"Come this way, Lanee. I want to give you your birthday present."

Carrying the interesting bundle, he walked me to a grassy spot away from the crowd. He helped me to sit down then he sat beside me and placed the package into my hands. "I hope you like it. It's my first gift to my wife, but, Lord willing, it surely won't be my last."

I smiled into his serious eyes and enjoyed seeing his smile move back into them. When I opened the cloth, I saw a beautifully crafted soft leather girdle. The natural color was just right for the tunic I was wearing. I was surprised. I liked it instantly and stood up to try it on. The straps wove into the slits in the girdle so that it fit snugly and comfortably on my waist. I smiled down at him when I had it fastened. When he saw that I liked it, he gave a relieved sigh and laughed.

"Did you make it for me, Ben?"

"Yes, with Yosef's help."

I pictured him bending over the soft leather trying to make something lovely for me, and suddenly I couldn't help saying, "Oh, Ben, I love you!"

He got up and took my hands in his. He bent his dark head and met my eyes—his were all soft with his feelings. He said, "I love you, too, Lanee."

Oh, sweetest of moments, please last forever!

"Hey, Ben! Lanee!"

We turned at the call. Then Ben smiled a goodbye for now, and I smiled back.

David was calling to us from the wagon that was harnessed to Chaff and Wheat. Yosef was bouncing up with David, Eema Lira, Savta, and with the back of the wagon full of food. They unloaded the women and the food then Yosef headed back to pick up Brothers James and Simon and their families, whom they had passed walking. Yosef had closed the inn, but this time had only left a sign that said, "Closed All Day Sunday."

Ben and I walked over to David. "Shalom, Ben! Happy birthday, Lanee!" His eyes sparkled as he greeted us. "My bucket of faith turned over again this morning—the Lord's about to do something!"

Ben and I stole a quick look at each other. *He already has, David!*

Then I said, "Oh, my! I remember last time!"

"Yes, may we have another day like that, Lord Jesus?" Ben said, remembering his baptism.

David peered anxiously down the road. "So ... Deborah's not here yet," he said. "But she will be." He stood where he could keep his eyes on the road, and as we talked, he watched.

Soon everyone had arrived, except Deborah and Brother Zibeon. Abba said we'd wait just a little longer before starting the service.

We three stood there and began praying quietly. I didn't know for sure, but it seemed David had shared his heart with Ben, too. We prayed and kept our eyes on the road, hoping to see a carriage flying toward us, with a big man driving and a pretty girl beside him.

Abba waded out into the water with Yosef following. We saw them and moved toward the lake, too.

"Lanee! David!" We all heard the small voice calling to us from the lake. We saw a boat coming toward us still a way off. As it came closer, we saw a huge man rowing it hard and a pretty girl standing up and waving. David ran into the lake and headed their way, and Ben followed him. I lifted my hands thanking God for His wondrous ways. Even Abba and

Yosef began wading out toward the boat. When they met, the men started pushing the boat as Brother Zibeon kept rowing. David reached in and lifted Deborah out and carried her to the bank, his handsome face glowing.

Abba and Yosef stepped up on the shore, as David put Deborah down. She said, "Brother Jonathan, may we join you? We've enjoyed our fishing trip, but could use a little rest. We *have* been fishing as you can see by our catch." She pointed to a bucket of fresh musht in the back of the boat.

Abba's eyes filled with compassion, and he nodded. I could see he understood that she wasn't trying to deceive her abba, but had sought *some* way to be able to come and be baptized.

When we finally settled down from the surprise, Abba waded out in the water and began to pray. "Dear Father, who has given us your Son to be our wonderful Savior, thank you for Him and His blessed salvation. Please smile upon our service and let it give you glory, in Jesus' name, Amen."

He looked up at the church and said, "All who want to proclaim to the world that Jesus is your Savior, please come to the shore to be baptized."

They lined up, with Brother James and his wife wading out first. "I baptize you in the name of the Father, and of the Son, and of the Holy Ghost," Abba said as he took Brother James under the water. We all shouted God's praise as he came up. He waited in the water as his wife went under. Then Brother Simon, his wife, and five little children waded in. The children loved the water, clapping and splashing all around as their brothers and sisters were baptized.

Next, a balding man who spoke with a soft gravelly voice stepped out into the water. He was one of the Magdala church.

His reserved expression gave way to a loud "Praise the Lord!" when Abba and Yosef took him under and brought him back up. Two young men from Magdala followed him one after the other. They both laughed and hugged Abba, Yosef, and each other. Only two were left in the line.

I saw Deborah asked Brother Zibeon to go first. He waded out and went under with Abba, Yosef, and David straining to hold him. When he came up shouting, they let go and let him shout. He shouted down and up in the water, all the time crying, "I'm free, Jesus! I'm free!" We all shouted with him.

Then it was Deborah's turn. She was wearing a thick embroidered tunic of blue and white. My eema instructed me about what to wear for modesty's sake when I was baptized. I admired Deborah's understanding it without the benefit of instruction. Wading out, she approached Abba with tears starting down her cheeks. David stepped up near her, and I saw he was crying, too. Abba waited for her to cross her arms and hold her nose then said, "I baptize you in the name of the ..."

"Stop!" a growling voice ordered from behind us.

Shocked, we all turned around. What shocked us even more was that it looked like the whole synagogue had come and were staring at us from the grass not even a stone's throw away.

Standing out in front, richly dressed Daniel ben Judah, Deborah's abba, commanded again, "Stop!"

Rabbi ben Tzadik, only a step behind him, looked angrier than I'd ever seen him.

CHAPTER TWENTY-SEVEN
OUR HERITAGE

"*Z*IBEON, get my daughter out of that water, and do it now!"

Brother Zibeon did not move.

"Zibeon, I heard you crying out 'I'm free!' You are not! You are my slave! I command you to bring my daughter up out of the lake now!"

Brother Zibeon did not move.

Deborah was still poised between Abba and Yosef's hands. Visibly shaken, she stared into her abba's eyes.

She pulled herself loose from his eyes and turned to look at me on her left. The sweet time we'd had in the flowered court when she met Jesus flooded my mind, and I sent her a smile. Her eyes moved to David near her in the lake, who gave her a tender, encouraging look. She swung her eyes to Ben beside me, who nodded his faith to her.

Then she started wading through the water toward her abba. David followed her. When she reached the shore, I joined them. I knew Ben was behind me. Out of the corner of my eye, I saw the rest of the church—Eema, Savta, Zia, Eema Lira—closing in behind us. Deborah stopped ten paces from her angry father.

"Abba? Abba. This is my opportunity to have the Lord God in my life. I am not satisfied just to talk about Him anymore. You must not hinder me from receiving my heritage from Him." Her lovely face turned up to her abba's proud face.

Hers seemed to match his in strength.

When she fell silent, David, cleared his voice of tears and spoke, "The psalmist asks you today, 'Let the children of Zion be joyful in their King.' We have felt the hand of God through His precious Son upon us, as we never did in the synagogues. We must have this life!"

Then Ben's firm steady voice began as soon as David finished, "The mighty God of Abraham, Isaac, and Jacob, who told Moses, I AM THAT I AM, is with us." He looked directly at his abba and eema. "He sent Jesus to redeem His people from their sins. Why will you not believe?" He turned his dark eyes on the rabbi. "Is it because the love of God is not in you?"

Then I felt the Holy Ghost filling my mouth, so I spoke, "'All we like sheep have gone astray; we have turned every one to his own way; and the Lord hath laid on him the iniquity of us all. He was oppressed, and he was afflicted, yet he opened not his mouth: he is brought as a lamb to the slaughter, and as a sheep before her shearers is dumb, so he openeth not his mouth. He was taken from prison and from judgment: and who shall declare his generation?'"

I looked into the crowd, seeing Mar Phinehas, the women I'd seen at the market, Misha, Elisabeth, and their parents. "We are declaring that we are His generation. We are Jews—as He is, and yes, we are your children, but, we will love Him—it is our heritage."

When I stopped, we all were quiet.

Then the rabbi stepped into the middle. He said, "I demand you children remember your place. Will you teach your elders? You are exhibiting just what I have been trying to stop in Arbela—rebellion against God's recognized authority. There will be no more baptizing in our village!" He stomped up closer to Abba and waved his finger under Abba's nose. "You must all get out, if you are not willing to give up Jesus of Nazareth and return to ..."

His voice trailed off when he saw his daughter, Sarah, walk past him, from the synagogue side to our side. She put her arm around Deborah and bowed her head.

"What are you doing, Sarah?" He looked at her with incredulous eyes, his face growing redder than his hair.

She lifted her head and looked up into his face. I could tell she was as scared as could be. Trembling, she said, "Abba, Lanee said God filled her up with His Spirit. I want that. Deborah told me yesterday, she doesn't feel mean and proud anymore. I want that. Lanee's abba is happy and loving. I want that. Deborah told me the songs they sing are sweet and all the words touch your heart. I want that."

Then I heard a strange rustling sound. It was people moving. Ben's abba and eema came to him. Deborah's beautiful eema took her husband's arm and walked him over to Deborah. He came willingly. Elisabeth came, and Misha, and their parents. Mar Phinehas and his wife came and stood with Eema. Then the most amazing thing of all happened—Rabbi ben Tzadik's wife moved up beside him, looked into his eyes for a long moment, shook her head, then walked over to Sarah and took her in her arms.

He glared at them for a horrible minute, then turned and stomped down the road alone. His elegant robe stretched over his rigid back. His hands were fists at the end of his stiff arms. They pumped at his sides faster and faster, matching

his strides, as he left us. The rest of the synagogue stood torn
between the two sides, and finally most of them straggled
back down the road too, after their rabbi.

We stood watching them as they drew farther and farther
away, then Abba stepped up and said, "Sister Deborah, are
you ready to be baptized?"

CHAPTER TWENTY-EIGHT

THE RABBI'S PROMISE

"RABBI?"

"Who's there?"

It was late afternoon, and the synagogue was a dark cavern, with no lamps lit yet.

"It's Lanee … uh … Jonathan's daughter."

"I know who you are. What do you want?"

He was standing behind the pulpit, looking out on the empty seats. I was at the door at the back of the meeting hall.

"I wondered if I might talk to you, Rabbi."

"Not if you're going to talk about that deceiver."

I'd hoped our prayers would help me get over this obstacle with him. *Help me, Jesus.*

"May I come in?"

"You haven't said what you want."

"I want to talk to you about a promise, Rabbi."

My hammering pulse was all I heard as several minutes passed. *Jesus, help him,* I prayed.

"All right. You may come up here and sit."

I was surprised. I walked into the familiar room and started down the center aisle, despairing at the noise my sandals were making. I sat down in the first row. He continued to stand behind the reading desk. Red hair framed a freckled face with a flame-colored beard. The hair and beard showed some gray in it now. His stocky build along with his more than average height made him seem unreachable to me.

Help me, Savior!

"Now, what is it?

Up close, I could see how the revered man's feelings were hurt and, oh, was he angry about it! How can I describe him? His jaw was clenched, his nose lifted, his eyes were inward and burning hot. I wanted to run out. *But, no, I must tell him.*

"I remember seeing you in Jerusalem on the day of Pentecost."

When he heard that, he turned his eyes on me. He hadn't looked at me before this. "You saw me?"

"Yes, I thought you knew I did. We were on the street praying for the people, and I saw you through the crowd."

"What *was* all that? I'd never heard of such public emotional displays and gibberish!"

"It was the coming of the promise."

"What 'promise'?" He bit the word off as if it tasted bitter in his mouth.

"The promise in the Book of Joel, Rabbi," I said meekly.

Again, the synagogue fell quiet.

I felt the touch of the Holy Ghost. I spoke, "And it shall come to pass afterward, that I will pour out my spirit upon all flesh; and your sons and your daughters shall prophesy, your old men shall dream dreams, your young men shall see visions: And also upon the servants and upon the handmaids in those days will I pour out my spirit."

My eyes held his while I spoke the Scriptures. I saw he recognized the words. I saw his jaw loosen a bit, and I saw the hot fire in his eyes cool some.

"Lanee, what do you know of such things? You are just a child." When he said it, I saw him remembering the words

I'd just quoted and look away from me.

"Why are you telling me this?"

"The promise is for you." As I said this, my eyes betrayed me—out came tears falling over my cheeks and down the front of my tunic. I didn't make a sound, but still he turned and fastened his burning eyes on me, "God loves you, Rabbi." was all I could say then, afraid that my public display of emotion had ruined it all.

Suddenly he looked down, and I saw two great tears roll down the sides of his nose. I heard him stomping his feet, one and then the other, and then I heard our rabbi lift his voice up above all the empty synagogue seats and me. "Lord God, I had given up! Bless me to help Your people, I used to cry. I had forgotten!" Then he sobbed.

It was almost dark now. I wasn't sure what to do. *Jesus, show me.*

"Lanee! Lanee! Where are you?" It was Abba calling from a distance. He must have come looking for me. I slipped out of my seat, down the aisle, and out of the synagogue door.

I ran back toward the well, and there he was! "Abba! Abba! Come with me! The rabbi is crying!"

Abba was astonished. He ran behind me to the synagogue. We heard his sobbing before we entered the door. Abba groaned when he saw him. The rabbi's head hung down between his arms braced on both sides of the pulpit.

Abba walked down the aisle and up beside him. He slipped his arm over his shoulder. His low rumbling praying joined the heart wrenching sobs of the rabbi.

I went up to Abba and whispered, "I'll go home and tell Eema." He nodded and continued praying.

Darkness had settled over our village. I walked by the well and remembered meeting my Ben there, and saw the palm Deborah sat under that day. I passed by Eema Lira and David's cottage. The rooms were lit, and I smelled the good supper she was cooking for them. On toward home I thought of Savta's healing, of Simon and James running after David to be saved, and of Sarah's scared voice saying, "I want it."

Oh yes, the promise of the Holy Ghost has come to our village, and He's brought along with Him every good thing God has. I took a long deep breath of the night air, lifted my sore heart toward Heaven, and whispered, *Thank you, Jesus.*

My Father's Business
Doing Business God's Way
by Peter Tsukahira

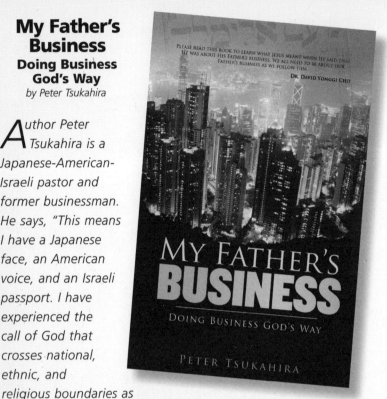

*A*uthor Peter
Tsukahira is a
Japanese-American-
Israeli pastor and
former businessman.
He says, "This means
I have a Japanese
face, an American
voice, and an Israeli
passport. I have
experienced the
call of God that
crosses national,
ethnic, and
religious boundaries as
I have lived, done business, and ministered in the United States,
Japan, and Israel." Peter now pastors on Mount Carmel, but he
was once an executive in a multinational computer company.
He wants people to know that God's calling is not limited to
ministry in the church; it includes the marketplace as well.
My Father's Business is organized into very readable, concise
chapters that will help the reader to become an agent of change
in society and the marketplace.

The POWER of the BUSINESS WORLD to ADVANCE GOD'S KINGDOM

ISBN: 978-088270-871-3
TPB / 172 pages

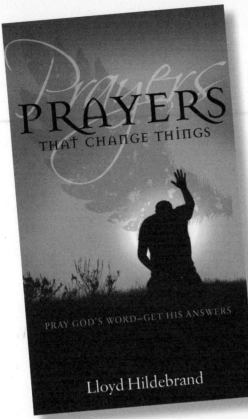

Prayers That Change Things
Pray God's Word— Get His Answers
by Lloyd Hildebrand

*P*rayers That *Change Things* is a new book by an established writer of books on prayer, Lloyd B. Hildebrand, who co-authored the very popular *Prayers That Prevail* series, *Bible Prayers for All Your Needs*, *Praying the Psalms*, *Healing Prayers*, and several others. This new book contains prayers about personal feelings and situations, prayers that are built directly from the Bible. The reader will discover that praying the Scriptures will truly bring about changes to so many things, especially their outlook on life and the circumstances of life. These life-imparting, life-generating, life-giving, and life-sustaining prayers are sure to bring God's answers to meet the believer's needs. Pray them from your heart; then wait for God to speak to you. Remember, He always speaks through His Word.

This revolutionary approach joins the power of prayer with the power of God's Word.

ISBN: 978-1-61036-105-7
MM / 192 pages

Bridge Logos

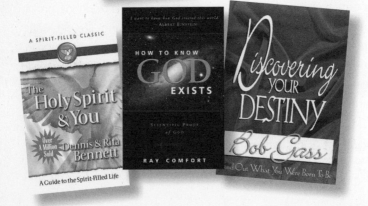

Top 20

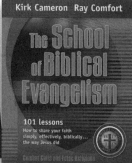

Over 2 Million Copies Sold

RUN BABY RUN

The Explosive True Story of a Savage Street Fighter

NICKY CRUZ
with Jamie Buckingham

Kirk Cameron   Ray Comfort

The School of Biblical Evangelism

101 lessons

How to share your faith simply, effectively, biblically... the way Jesus did

Combat Cults and False Religions

RAY COMFORT

SCIENTIFIC FACTS in the BIBLE

100 REASONS TO BELIEVE THE BIBLE IS SUPERNATURAL IN ORIGIN

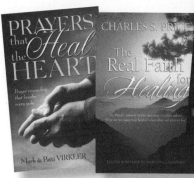

PRAYERS that Heal the HEART

Prayer counsels that breaks every yoke

Mark & Patti VIRKLER

CHARLES S. PRICE

The Real Faith for Healing

EDITED & REVISED BY HAROLD L. CHADWICK

BOOK 1 in the Keys of the Kingdom Trilogy

SHATTERING YOUR STRONGHOLDS

UPDATED AND EXPANDED

Liberty Savard

SUCCESSFUL HOME CELL GROUPS

BEST SELLER

From the Pastor of the World's Largest Church

Dr. David Yonggi Cho
with Harold Hostetler

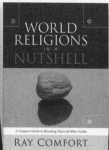
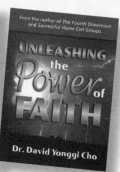

RAY COMFORT

The Way of the Master

Foreword and Commentary by KIRK CAMERON

Revised and Expanded. Over 100,000 in print. Free "Hell's Best Kept Secret" audio CD enclosed.

WORLD RELIGIONS IN A NUTSHELL

A Compact Guide to Reaching Those of Other Faiths

RAY COMFORT

From the author of The Fourth Dimension and Successful Home Cell Groups

UNLEASHING the Power of FAITH

Dr. David Yonggi Cho

Pure Gold Classics
Timeless Truth in a
Distinctive, Best-Selling Collection

- Illustrations
  - Detailed index
    - Author biography
      - In-depth Bible study
        - Expanding Collection—40-plus titles
          - Sensitively Revised in Modern English

AN EXPANDING COLLECTION
OF THE BEST-LOVED
CHRISTIAN CLASSICS
OF ALL TIME.

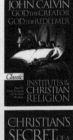

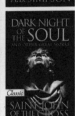

GOD OF ALL COMFORT — HANNAH WHITALL SMITH

THE GREATEST THING IN THE WORLD — HENRY DRUMMOND

THE IMITATION OF CHRIST — THOMAS à KEMPIS

IN HIS STEPS — CHARLES M. SHELDON

INTERIOR CASTLE — TERESA OF AVILA

THE HOLY SPIRIT POWER — JOHN WESLEY

R. A. TORREY — THE HOLY SPIRIT: WHO HE IS AND WHAT HE DOES

HUMILITY — ANDREW MURRAY

JEWELS FROM E. M. BOUNDS — E. M. BOUNDS

THE KNEELING CHRISTIAN — AN UNKNOWN CHRISTIAN

MADAME JEANNE GUYON

MORNING BY MORNING — CHARLES H. SPURGEON

THE OVERCOMING LIFE — D. L. MOODY

THE PILGRIM'S PROGRESS IN MODERN ENGLISH — JOHN BUNYAN

POWER, PASSION & PRAYER — CHARLES G. FINNEY

THE PRACTICE OF THE PRESENCE OF GOD — BROTHER LAWRENCE

SECRET POWER — D. L. MOODY

A SERIOUS CALL TO A DEVOUT & HOLY LIFE — WILLIAM LAW

THE SERMON ON THE MOUNT — JOHN WESLEY

SINNERS IN THE HANDS OF AN ANGRY GOD — JONATHAN EDWARDS

THE SOVEREIGNTY OF GOD — A. W. PINK

SPURGEON ON THE HOLY SPIRIT — CHARLES H. SPURGEON

SPURGEON ON PRAYER — CHARLES H. SPURGEON

TABLE TALK — MARTIN LUTHER

TORREY ON PRAYER — THE POWER OF PRAYER & THE PRAYER OF POWER

TOZER — FELLOWSHIP OF THE BURNING HEART

TOZER: MYSTERY OF THE HOLY SPIRIT — A. W. TOZER

WALKING WITH GOD — THE ANDREW MURRAY TRILOGY ON SANCTIFICATION

WILLIAM WILBERFORCE — GREATEST WORKS

WITH CHRIST IN THE SCHOOL OF PRAYER — ANDREW MURRAY

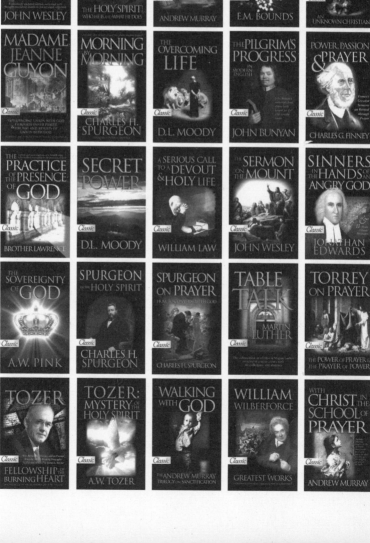
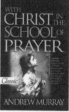